"You frightened me!"
she cried accusingly

"I wasn't aware that I had to inform my aunt's companion of my whereabouts." Alexander's voice was silky.

"What a perfectly beastly thing to say—and very rude besides!" Jemima's temper was rising.

"I'll apologize if it will make you happy, Jemima. I can only say that you have the unfortunate effect of bringing out the very worst in me." Alexander looked at her with the faintest of smiles. "You would do better to avoid me."

She was retreating slowly backward. "Me avoid you? I've never gone looking for you, you know. But I'll do my best in future."

He really smiled then. "You're quite a treasure, Jemima. We must keep you in the family."

"In your nasty arrogant way I suppose you mean that kindly. However, nothing on earth could induce me to stay...."

BETTY NEELS

is also the author of these

Harlequin Romances

Many of these books are available at your local bookseller.

For a free catalog listing all titles currently available,
send your name and address to:

HARLEQUIN READER SERVICE
1440 South Priest Drive, Tempe, AZ 85281
Canadian address: Stratford, Ontario N5A 6W2

A Dream Came True

Betty Neels

Harlequin Books

TORONTO • NEW YORK • LOS ANGELES • LONDON
AMSTERDAM • PARIS • SYDNEY • HAMBURG
STOCKHOLM • ATHENS • TOKYO • MILAN

Original hardcover edition published in 1982
by Mills & Boon Limited

ISBN 0-373-02550-5

Harlequin Romance first edition May 1983

Printed in U.S.A.

CHAPTER ONE

THE room was small and shabby, but comfortable enough, with the firelight flickering on the unimaginative furniture and the small table with the remains of a meal upon it. Two people were sitting there, a young man with a thin, spectacled face and a girl somewhat older, with straight shoulder-length mousy fair hair and a face which just missed being pretty by reason of a slightly turned up nose and a too wide mouth. But the mouth curved gently and her eyes, hazel and thickly fringed, were quite beautiful. She sat very quietly, her hands, small and capable and a little roughened from housework, clasped loosely on the table before her. When she spoke her voice was brisk but pleasantly soft.

'Well, love, that's settled, then. We'll give up this flat—I never liked it much, did you? You go off to Boston and I'll find a job to keep me going until you come home again,' and when her brother made an impatient gesture: 'No, Dick, it's no good arguing any more, it's a heavensent chance for you and you simply must take it, and what's two years? You'll only be twenty-three . . .' she ignored his muttered 'And you'll be twenty-eight,' and went on firmly: 'You'll probably be a famous scientist by then and we'll live in a nice house in the country and I'll keep hens . . .'

'But that's years away, Jemima—what's going to happen to you in the meantime?' He sighed heavily. 'You're not trained for anything, are you?'

Rather like a magician she produced a folded news-

5

paper and passed it to him. 'Read that,' she begged him, and tapped the advertisements column. I'm cut out for it—I shall go there tomorrow.'

Her brother read it, frowning. 'But this wouldn't do—it's drudgery!'

'Rubbish.' If her voice faltered a little he didn't notice it. 'I've walked dogs all my life, haven't I, and read aloud to Mother and Father every day for years, I can answer the phone intelligently and write letters and play cards. I shall do very nicely. It'll be an old dame with a Peke and a hearing aid—and the money is good.'

She got up, a girl not much above middle height and rather on the plump side, and began to clear the table.

'I've got to get your suit from the cleaners and fetch your shoes. Will you have enough money until they pay you?'

'I'll manage; I shan't know anyone to start with, shall I? Besides, I plan to work.'

'Yes, love, but you can't work all the time. I wonder what Boston is like? America for that matter—mind you write at least once a month.' She grinned at him. 'And take most of what's left in the bank just to be on the safe side.'

'What about you?'

'Oh, I'll do fine. I've enough clothes and there'll be enough to keep me going until I get my wages. It says "Good salary" and if I live in I'll not have a care in the world.' Jemima spoke cheerfully and inwardly contemplated the future with some doubt; she was a practical girl, not given to moaning or wanting the moon, but she did wish that she had been trained to do something. But there had been no need—her parents had assured her of that each time she had brought the subject up. Her father was a Professor of

History at one of the colleges at Oxford, living in a delightful old house which went with the job, and her mother had been only too delighted to leave more and more of the housekeeping to her. And she hadn't complained; she had a small allowance, a number of friends and no prospect of marrying; she was neither clever enough nor pretty enough to catch the eye of younger men, and the older ones were all married. She hoped that one day she would marry, but here she was, twenty-six last birthday and apart from a middle-aged don, a widower with three teenage children, no proposals. And for the last four years she hadn't minded at all. When her father died her mother had somehow lost her zest for living too, and Jemima had taken over the running of the house, the paying of the bills and the shopping, not thinking too much about the future. Authority had allowed them to stay on in the house which had been their home for so long and Dick had finished his studies and done brilliantly and somehow she had managed very well on the pension which they now lived on. But when her mother died suddenly, life changed drastically. They had to leave their home; there was no more pension and only a very little money left in the bank. They had sold the furniture and moved into a poky little flat so that Dick could continue his studies while he waited to see if he had won a place at Boston University, where he would have a grant sufficient to keep him while he worked for still another degree. He had done even better; he had been offered a place there with the prospect of a good job at the end of it, and Jemima had urged him to snap it up, brushing aside his doubts about her own future.

All the same, she had scoured the advertisements for several weeks now trying to find something which would suit her few talents, and at last something had turned up and she had every intention of applying for it. The advertisement stipulated an interview, in the first instance at an address in Bloomsbury. She had looked it up and found it to be a street close to the British Museum, a fairly familiar ground to her, for she had been there on several occasions with her father. It sounded very respectable.

She went up to London on a morning train. The interviews were timed for three o'clock and she supposed there might be several girls there as well as herself; she would get there exactly on the hour and in the meantime do a little window-shopping, have a snack lunch and make her way on foot to the address in the advertisement. It was a pleasant day in late September, when she considered London was at its best, and she spent an hour or so going unhurriedly from one big store to the next. If she got the job she would be able to buy one or two things to bring her wardrobe up to date—she made a list while she drank coffee and ate a dull ham sandwich, and then walked on, away from the shops now, taking short cuts through narrow streets full of people hurrying out for their lunch, until she arrived in front of the British Museum. Here she had to stop and ask someone the way, and presently found herself in a quiet Bloomsbury square, its tall houses overlooking the garden in its centre. Number ninety-one would be at the far end; she started to walk along one side, noting that almost all the houses had brass plates under their old-fashioned brass bells—offices, she supposed, lawyers, dentists and doctors, she imagined with some satisfaction, so even more respectable than she had hoped for.

Number ninety-one's front door stood open, so Jemima went into the lobby and from there into a narrow hall and followed an arrow on the wall which had 'Waiting Room' written under it, and found another door on the landing above, a handsome mahogany one with 'Waiting Room' on a discreet brass plate. No one answered when she knocked and since a nearby church clock was striking the hour, she opened the door and went inside.

The room wasn't large, but it was empty of people, which rather surprised her. She glanced at the address again to make sure that she had come to the right place and then went and sat down. There were a couple of small easy chairs against one wall, but she chose the straight-backed chair behind the desk set cornerwise against the window, where she sat composedly, waiting.

She waited for ten minutes and no one appeared; held up by traffic, she decided, and getting bored, typed her name with one finger on the paper ready in the typewriter and, flushed with this success, carefully filled in the rest of the line with the first thing which came into her head: 'Little Jack Horner sat in a corner——' She came to the end of the paper and turned the roller, quite absorbed. She had a finger poised for the next word when there was a quick determined step on the stairs and the door was opened.

Jemima froze in her chair, not daring to look up. Suppose it was the typist whose machine she was messing about with? She put her hands in her lap and assumed what she hoped was a serene expression.

The steps had reached the desk and she looked up, just in time to have a sheaf of papers thrust at her and hear a deep impatient voice say: 'Get these typed by five o'clock, will you?' He barely glanced at her. 'I suppose you're the girl from the typing pool to replace Miss Ames? I hope you're efficient.'

Jemima goggled at him, looking, if only she knew,

the height of inefficiency. She had to tell him smartly that he was mistaken, but she hesitated for a few seconds because she really had to look at him. Tall and very large, with pepper-and-salt hair and the coldest grey eyes she had ever seen; a mouth pressed into a thin line and a high-bridged nose—very nice-looking if only he'd smile . . . She opened her mouth finally. 'I . . .' she began, too late as he strode past her and went through a door at the end of the room, closing it with a decided click which somehow prevented her from following him.

She looked at the papers he had given her—not even ordinary writing but page upon page of what looked like Greek and little sums dotted here and there—a kind of advanced algebra, perhaps? She looked at it for a minute or two, summoning up courage to go after him and explain, vexed with herself because she felt timid and nervous. 'Ridiculous,' she said out loud. 'Father always said you had more common sense in your little finger than any other female he'd ever known.'

She tidied the papers into a neat pile and prepared so stand up just as the door opened again. This time it was a girl, a gorgeous creature with golden hair, a fetching waistcoat and black velvet knickerbockers. She swanned in, smiled brilliantly at Jemima and draped herself in one of the chairs.

'Hullo—is he in?'

Jemima nodded while she wondered if her legs were good enough to carry off knickerbockers. She was probably far too curvy, she thought regretfully.

'Oh, good. Be a darling and tell him I'm here, will you?'

It was a chance to see the man and explain. Jemima got to her feet once more, the papers in her hand. 'What name?' she asked.

'Just say Gloria.'

She knocked on the door before she had time to get nervous and walked in. The man was sitting at a massive desk, his head bowed over a pile of papers, so untidy that Jemima itched to straighten them.

'There's a young lady,' she began, and encouraged by his grunt: 'Her name is Gloria . . .'

'Tell her to go away—I shan't be ready for hours yet. How's that typing going?'

He looked up and his eyes narrowed as he caught sight of the papers.

'Well,' said Jemima, reasonably, 'not very well, I'm afraid. You see, I can't type . . .'

'Then why the hell are you here?' He flung a hand on to the desk so violently that most of the papers there flew on to the floor. 'Now look what you've done!' he declared furiously.

'Not me—you,' Jemima corrected him calmly. 'If you wouldn't get so cross I could explain.'

'I am not cross. Well?'

She explained with commendable brevity while he sat glowering at her. 'So,' she concluded matter-of-factly, 'if you would tell me where I ought to be . . . it does give this address, you know.'

He frowned at her. 'Sit down, wait here,' he told her, and went out. She could hear his voice rumbling on about something or other and Gloria's rather shrill tones interrupting. Presently a door banged and he came back.

'You appear to be the only applicant for the post,' he said without preamble, 'but I don't imagine you will get it. The lady in question is difficult to please; I don't think you are suitable.' His cold eyes studied her leisurely and she said tartly:

'Don't stare, it's rude, and what has it got to do with you, anyway?'

Just for a moment the grey eyes warmed with amusement. 'Er—nothing. I merely suggest that you might not be able to cope—a companion's life isn't all roses.'

'I didn't expect it to be. And now perhaps you will be good enough to tell me where I should go?'

'Perhaps I am mistaken—appearances are so deceptive. Take a taxi to this address'—he was scribbling on a pad as he spoke. 'It's close to Harrods—you will of course be reimbursed for any expenses.'

Jemima stood up, took the paper he was offering her, wished him good afternoon, and went to the door. He hadn't answered her, hadn't looked up even. She said as she opened the door, 'You'll have to do your own typing, won't you?'

Sitting in the taxi she was filled with remorse and shame; to have been so rude, and such a waste too—a complete stranger she would never see again, but it was no good brooding about it, she still had to get the job. 'Not suitable, indeed!' she muttered, and when the taxi stopped in a quiet street in Knightsbridge, she had got out, paid her fare, added a tip and mounted the steps to the front door of the tall narrow house, thumped the door with the heavy brass knocker, and when it was opened, trod firmly through it.

The man she had given her name to was short and stout and puffed a good deal. He said civilly: 'If you would come this way, miss,' and led her across a high-ceilinged hall to a small room, where he begged her to sit down and then shut the door firmly upon her. It was a pleasant place, nicely warm and well furnished, and she sat back comfortably and thought longingly of her tea—perhaps she would be offered a cup? If not she could stop on her way to the station. Her musings were interrupted by the stout man, who appeared silently and asked her to follow him, this time up the curved saircase and on to a broad landing with a number of doors. He opened one of these and ushered her inside. 'Miss Mason, my lady,' he intoned, and shut the door behind her.

'Well, come in, come in,' said an impatient voice from the other end of a large lofty room, and Jemima advanced across the beeswaxed floor, over a beautiful Indian carpet, avoiding chairs, little tables and enormous sofas, until she reached the wing chair by the window where an old lady was sitting.

'Stand there,' she commanded, 'where I can see you—I can't say you're much to look at.'

To which Jemima made no answer; she could have agreed, of course, but she saw no reason to do so. The old lady went on: 'I am Lady Manderly. I suppose you are applying for the post of companion?'

'Yes, I am.' Jemima wasn't sure whether she should say my lady or Lady Manderly, so she chose Lady Manderly, then stood quietly, taking a good look at her companion. Lady Manderly was an imposing figure, even though an outsize one, with a formidable bosom encased in a beautifully tailored grey wool dress in the style made fashionable by Queen Mary. Her iron-grey hair was dressed in a fashion which Jemima decided was vaguely Edwardian, and she wore a magnificent choker of jet beads and gold, supporting a series of quivering chins. From somewhere about her person she produced a lorgnette and studied Jemima at length and in silence.

Jemima bore the scrutiny with calm for a minute or so and then said kindly: 'You would be much more comfortable with glasses, Lady Manderly.'

The lorgnette was lowered and two hard grey eyes glared at her. They reminded her forcibly of the man who had interviewed her earlier with such abruptness.

Somewhere under that Gorgon front, thought Jemima, there must be a nice old lady lurking. Apparently not. 'I will not tolerate impertinence,' declared Lady Manderly.

'I wasn't being impertinent, Lady Manderly. An aunt of mine always used a lorgnette until she was persuaded to change to ordinary glasses; she found them a great deal better than forever fidgeting with a lorgnette.'

'I do not fidget,' observed Lady Manderly awfully. 'What experience have you had?'

'Well, actually none at all, but I can read aloud, and play most card games and answer the telephone sensibly, and write letters. I'm very strong too.' Jemima frowned a little. 'Oh, and I can drive a car and run a house economically. My mother became ill after my father died, so I saw to everything . . .'

'I have a housekeeper, a butler and a number of servants, Miss—er—Mason. I am, I consider, a considerate and generous employer. You are not quite the type I would have wished for, but since no one else has applied, I will offer you the post on a month's approval. You will live out; I can't have the servants running round after you morning and evening—and I will give you forty pounds a week wages.'

Jemima said gently: 'I should have been glad to accept, Lady Manderly, but if I have to live out I can't possibly live on that amount. Clothes and shoes and things,' she added matter-of-factly. 'I won't take up any more of your time. Good afternoon, Lady Manderly.'

She started for the door, indeed she had a hand on

the door handle when Lady Manderly spoke. 'I will give you fifty pounds a week, Miss Mason—that is a generous offer. You will come here each morning from nine o'clock and remain until six o'clock in the evening. You will, of course, have your lunch here and your tea. I shall not require you on Sundays.'

'I should need a half day each week—shopping for food and seeing my friends.'

Lady Manderly sighed so deeply that Jemima expected to see the seams of her dress give way. 'You are like all modern young women, selfish and indifferent to the comfort of others. You may have a half day each week. Be good enough to start your duties on Monday next. You have references?'

Jemima handed over the names and addresses of some elderly friends of her parents.

'If they are not satisfactory I will let you know. Be good enough to give your address to my butler as you go out.' Lady Manderly nodded regally and Jemima, not in the least intimidated, whisked herself out of the room and down the stairs to encounter the butler in the hall.

He wrote down her address impassively and then puffed his way to the front door and held it open for her. 'I trust we shall see you in due course, miss,' he observed, and allowed his features to relax into the beginnings of a small smile.

'Me too,' said Jemima.

So far so good, she thought as she walked briskly towards the end of the square. Now to find somewhere to live; close by and cheap. The main road was bustling with people and traffic, another world to the peace and dignity which she had just left. There were shops here, mostly good class boutiques, high class grocers and the kind of greengrocer who sold out-of-season fruit and vegetables, but tucked in between them, her searching eye saw a stationers and post office. A likely place to enquire for rooms, she considered. She crossed the street and made her way there and since the shop was almost empty, she went inside.

A redhaired young woman behind the post office counter listened to her silently. 'Well, I might know of something,' she observed in a cheerful cockney voice, 'and then again I might not.' She eyed Jemima's sober appearance. 'What do you do?'

'Well, I've just got a job as a daily companion. I'd only want a room and bed and breakfast.'

The girl chewed on a pencil. 'There's a room 'ere,' she said at length. 'Me mum lives over the shop and she likes a lodger.' She opened the counter flap. 'You'd better come up and see 'er.'

Mum was small and wiry and sharp-tongued, but her eyes were kind. 'It ain't much of a room,' she said, but with no hint of apology, 'but it's clean and it's got a gas fire and a ring for yer kettle, there's a wash basin too, but yer'll 'ave ter use the loo at the end of the passage.'

It was a dim little room with a view of chimney pots and a strip of sky, but the furniture wasn't too bad; there was a small table under the window and a rather battered armchair, a wardrobe and bookshelves and a bed against one wall. With her own small possessions and an eiderdown and a few flowers, Jemima decided, it would do. And the rent was no more than she could afford to pay. Panic caught her by the throat when she remembered that she would be here for two years perhaps, but she made herself forget that. She said steadily: 'It's very nice, I should like to take it. You'd like some rent in advance, wouldn't you—and references?'

'I'll have a week's money, dear, but I know a lady when I see one—I don't need no references.' The girl added sharply: 'Name's Adams—Mrs Adams. Come into me sitting room and 'ave a cup of tea.'

Jemima drank dark sweet tea thankfully, it was just what she needed. She listened to Mrs Adams telling her about hot water for baths, what kind of breakfast she would get and how the gas fire was on its own meter and she'd have to pay for it separately. 'And if you want ter cook yerself a snack I've no objection. Yer'll get yer breakfast later on a Sunday, me and Shirley like a nice lie-in. Yer'll eat in 'ere. If yer want the milkman or the baker, I'll take in yer stuff. There's a launderette down Smith Street, that's first right when you go out of the shop.' She gave Jemima a quick look. 'Yer can do yer smalls in the bathroom, but don't 'ang em there.'

Jemima promised that she wouldn't, finished her tea, parted with a weeks rent and said goodbye. 'If I could move in on Sunday evening?' she asked. 'I have to work from nine to six o'clock and I'd like to get settled in first.'

Mrs Adams nodded. 'O.K. Ring the shop door bell twice so that we know who it is.'

Jemima had to wait for a train; she sat on the station, impervious to the crowds of homegoing people milling around her, doing careful arithmetic on the back of an envelope. She would be able to manage nicely if she were careful; she had clothes enough, not very new, but they had been good when she had bought them, she would have to allow for tights and soap and writing paper and stamps and all the small things one overlooked normally, but she would have no fares and, with luck, a good lunch every day, she might even save a little money. She went on with her sums when she was in the train and by the time she reached the flat at Oxford, she was her usual calm cheerful self. After all, she had the job, she had somewhere to live and in two years time Dick would be back in England and they could set up house together and if, as he was bound to do, Dick married, she would learn typing and short-hand and become some powerful executive's right hand secretary. It would be nice to marry, of course, but she didn't dwell on that; she was after all turned twenty-six and no beauty.

Dick was home, deep in his books, which he had spread out all over the table. Jemima took off her jacket, piled them tidily and laid the table for their supper. She had been busy about this for a minute or two before he looked up to ask: 'Well, did you get the job?'

'Yes, and I think I'll quite enjoy it too. I have to live out, but I've found a very nice bedsitter close by—it's just behind Harrod's—her name is Lady Manderly.'

'That's splendid—is she paying you enough?'

'Quite enough, love. I shall manage splendidly. I'm to start on Monday, which is just right, isn't it? I'll be able to see you off on Sunday morning.' She smiled a little ruefully as she spoke; Dick had already turned back to his book, obviously relieved that her future had been settled so easily.

Perhaps it was a good thing that he was going to America on his own, she reflected, watching the plane getting smaller and smaller as it left Heathrow. He had always been looked after—not spoilt, she told herself, he was too nice for that, but since an early age he had buried his head in books; food and clothes, even people, had meant very little to him. She hoped that they would be kind to him in Boston, he was a nice boy and everyone liked him. She was going to miss him.

She spent the rest of the day cleaning the flat, handing over the keys and packing the rest of her things and in the evening she called a taxi and had herself driven to catch the train to her new home.

Mrs Adams answered the door, took one of her cases from her and ushered her upstairs. The flat smelled of Sunday dinner, but her room was spotlessly clean and the bed looked inviting. Left to herself Jemima lighted the gas fire, made tea on the gas ring and started to unpack. She quite enjoyed arranging her possessions round the room, and the bed looked even better with her eiderdown on it and the reading lamp on the small table beside it. She had almost finished when Shirley knocked and came in. 'Got all you want?' she asked kindly. 'Mum says breakfast at eight o'clock—we open the shop at half past. The water's hot if you want a bath.'

She sat down on the bed and smoothed the eiderdown with a careful hand. 'Silk, ain't it? I bet you 'as a posh 'ome.'

Jemima closed the wardrobe door. 'Well, I suppose it was, but home's what you make it, isn't it? I've been in some very grand houses and they're just like museums, not home at all—now this is cosy . . .'

Shirley stared at her. 'Cor—you mean it too, don't you? Well, I never! Mind you, I'd hate to live anywhere else but London—deadly dull it must be.' She got up. 'You can call me Shirl,' she invited.

'Thank you, Shirl—call me Jemima if you like.'

'Sounds a funny name to me, but if it's all you've got I'll 'ave to, won't I? So long.'

Jemima slept soundly. She was a sensible girl; Dick was safely embarked on a career, she had a job and a roof over her head and she didn't owe anyone any money, so there was no reason why she should stay awake.

She was up and ready for breakfast in good time, very neat in the navy blue suit she had worn to the interview. It was by no means new, but her shoes were good and her blouse, a white silk one she had had for years, dateless. Looking at her reflection in the mirror behind the wardrobe door, she hoped that her appearance was right for the job and was encouraged to think so by Mrs Adams, who put a plate of bacon and egg in front of her remarking: 'There's nothing like navy blue to make a girl look ladylike.' She poured strong tea and handed it to Jemima. 'Nervous?'

Jemima thought for a moment. 'Yes, I think I am, a little. I've never had a job before.'

'You'll do,' observed Shirley through a mouthful of toast and marmalade. 'Just remember not to let 'er sit on you—you stand up for yourself, see?' She pushed her chair back. 'Well, I'll go and get started, I suppose. You coming down later, Mum?'

Mrs Adams nodded. 'Yes, and just you see that that Ned does the till proper.' And as her daughter clattered down the stairs. ''E's the assistant part-time, but 'e's not much use.'

It was barely five minutes' walk to Lady Manderly's house. Jemima went back to her room, made the bed neatly, tidied it, picked up her bag and gloves and wished Mrs Adams goodbye. And in the shop Shirley sorting magazines with lightning efficiency, cried: 'Good luck, girl!' and waved airily from behind the counter. Jemima, outside on the pavement, found herself reluctant to cross the road; the little shop already seemed a safe shelter. She would be coming back that evening, she reminded herself, and nipped on to the opposite pavement, heading for Lady Manderly's house.

The door was opened by the same stout man and after wishing him a good morning, Jemima said: 'Will you tell me your name? I wasn't told the other day when I was here, but if we are going to see each other every day it would be nicer.' She smiled at him and he smiled back at her in a rather surprised way. 'Belling, miss. And I'm sure I hope you'll be happy here.'

'Why, thank you, Belling, I hope so too. What do I do next?'

'I'll show you the cloak room, miss, where you can put your things and then ascertain if Lady Manderly is ready for you.'

He started off across the hall and then paused as someone came running down the staircase. Jemima paused too, having no choice as a man came round the curve of the staircase. She recognised him at once— who could forget that pepper-and-salt hair and the size of him? He stopped as he reached them, nodded at Belling and stared hard at her. 'So you landed the job,' he observed. 'Well, I hope you'll be a better companion than you were a typist.' He smiled mockingly, but his eyes were as cold as the first time they had met.

Belling had gone to open the street door and he went through it without saying anything more. A very unpleasant man, but there was no harm in finding out who he was.

As Belling rejoined her she asked diffidently: 'That gentleman—we met the other day at his office . . .' She allowed her voice to sound questioning and the butler answered readily enough.

'That is Professor Cator, miss—Professor Alexander Cator, Lady Manderly's nephew and a very famous man in his field of learning.

'Oh, what sort of learning?'

'Endocrinology, miss. He's considered to be a very clever gentleman.'

And a nasty bad-tempered one too, thought Jemima as she was ushered into the small room she had waited in on her first visit. It was a good ten minutes before Belling came back and asked her to follow him.

Jemima got up with alacrity. It was, after all, an important moment in her life; she was about to start her first job.

CHAPTER TWO

BELLING led the way upstairs and on to the landing, but this time he ignored the drawing-room door and knocked on a smaller door opposite, opened it and stood aside for Jemima to go past him. Compared to the drawing-room, the apartment she entered was small; it was also austerely furnished with a fine knee-hole writing desk, an upright chair behind it, a couple of small tables and an upholstered armchair drawn up to the small fire burning in the polished steel grate.

Lady Manderly was in the chair, wearing a dress exactly the same as the grey one, but this time it was blue and the jet and gold necklace had been replaced by a turquoise choker. There was a pile of letters on the small table by her chair and she was tapping impatiently with a beringed hand upon the newspaper on her lap.

Jemima wished her good morning politely and waited.

'I said nine o'clock,' began Lady Manderly icily.

'Yes, you did,' agreed Jemima pleasantly, 'and I was here at five minutes to the hour, Lady Manderly. I waited downstairs until Belling came to fetch me.' She glanced at the clock. 'For ten minutes,' she added.

Lady Manderly looked affronted. 'I am not always ready, Miss Mason. You will go through these letters and give me those which are personal so that I may read them. Bills, requests for money and so on you will put on the desk and consult me about them when it is convenient.' She added: 'To me.'

And when Jemima had done that: 'While I am reading my letters and when you have sorted the remainder, you will scan *The Times* and mark anything of significance so that you may read it to me during the course of the day.'

They settled down the pair of them, Lady Manderly occasionally making indignant noises over her correspondence, Jemima working silently, making a neat pile on the desk and then looking through the paper for likely bits to read—a formidable task, since she had no idea what the lady's tastes were; would she want to hear the Prime Minister's speech on the coal industry, or what the Middle East was doing at the moment? Or would she be interested in the fashion page? Jemima thought it unlikely; fashion as such didn't appear to mean much to her employer—she fancied that she made her own. She might like the social column, though, and the weather report . . .

Lady Manderly laid down the last of her letters. 'And now you may tell me about the rest,' she commanded.

They were mostly bills, but there were a couple of begging letters, a leaflet about thermal underwear, an enquiry as to whether Lady Manderly would like double glazing and a catalogue from Liberty's. Lady

Manderly made short work of them while Jemima scribbled little notes on each of them so that she would remember what she had to do later on.

'Now you may read to me,' stated Lady Manderly.

Jemima began with the weather report, touched lightly on the Middle East, read the whole of the Prime Minister's speech in full, added an item or two about the Royal Family's daily round, touched delicately upon the separation of a peer of the realm and his wife, and ended with a colourful account of the discovery of a rare ceramic—an Imari cat—which had been found on the kitchen overmantel in a Norfolk farmhouse.

As she folded the newspaper Lady Manderly remarked: 'You have a pleasant voice, Miss Mason, and your choice of reading material was most suitable. Kindly ring the bell for coffee.'

Coffee came, on a massive silver tray. Jemima poured it from a George the Second silver coffee pot into paper-thin cups, and it was atrocious—watery and bitter and not as hot as it should have been; she waited for Lady Manderly to complain, but that lady drank two cups with apparent enjoyment before desiring Jemima to ring the bell once more.

'You will take Coco for a walk and bring her back to me in one hour,' said Lady Manderly. 'My maid, Pooley, always takes her to St James' Park, but of course she has to be driven there and back. You, I presume, are young enough to enjoy a good walk.'

'Yes, of course I am, Lady Manderly, but what about Coco? Is she young?'

'Five—no, six years old, I believe. She does not, of course, get the exercise she should, so you may have to carry her if she tires.'

Jemima pictured herself struggling under the weight of a Great Dane. 'What sort of dog?' she asked.

'A poodle—miniature, of course. You may go now, Miss Mason, but be back at noon precisely.'

Belling was waiting in the hall when Jemima went downstairs, holding the lead of a very small grey poodle. 'The little dog is very good, miss,' he volunteered, 'she'll be glad of a nice walk.'

The sun was shining although there was a cool wind with a decided autumnal nip to it; just right for a brisk walk. The hour passed too quickly for both Jemima and Coco and she hoped that a daily walk was to be part of her duties. Coco, her paws wiped by a woman in an apron, summoned to the hall by Belling, was allowed to mount the stairs with Jemima and go into the drawing-room where Lady Manderly was sitting before a vast embroidery frame. She looked at her watch before she spoke. 'At least you are punctual,' she observed tartly. 'We lunch at one o'clock, until then you may start on the letters, and I have left you a list of telephone calls I wish you to make.' She pushed the frame aside. 'Come to Mother,' she begged Coco in such a different, gentle voice that Jemima stared. Perhaps Lady Manderly wasn't as harsh as she seemed. She went back to the small room and sat down at the desk. Fifty pounds had seemed an awful lot of money when she had been offered that sum; she saw now that she was going to earn every penny of it.

She quite enjoyed the next hour, however, telephoning for flowers to be sent, a fitter to come that afternoon with a new dress Lady Manderly had ordered, a wine merchant to deliver a dozen bottles of claret, and then settling down to write answers to the bills and begging letters in her neat handwriting. She made out cheques too, and when they were done, took them back to the drawing-room for Lady Manderly to sign. And by then it was lunch time.

Jemima was relieved to find that this was a substantial meal, which meant that she need only get herself a sandwich or beans on toast or an egg in the evening, and since Lady Manderly had a good appetite, she was able to enjoy her lunch down to the last mouthful. The coffee was frightful, though, and Jemima made up her mind to do something about that just as soon as she had got to know the members of the household.

Lady Manderly rested after lunch, she told Jemima, and liked to be read to, so Jemima made her comfortable on the day bed, draped a series of shawls around her massive person, and took a chair close by. She was to read one of Agatha Christie's earlier books, one she had read at least twice herself. She had got as far as the second chapter when she was brought up short by a tremendous snore from her companion. There was no point in going on, so she marked the place carefully and sat back in her chair, glad of a few minutes' quiet. So far, she thought, she wasn't doing too badly. Lady Manderly had watched her like a hawk during lunch, presumably to make sure that she knew which knives and forks to use, but she hadn't actually grumbled once. The thought that the job was going to bore her to tears within a month she stifled at once; she was lucky to get work and until she could train for something else she hadn't much choice.

Lady Manderly woke presently and Jemima went on reading, just as though she had never left off. Coco had to be taken for a short walk before four o'clock tea, a welcome break before Jemima found herself behind the silver tea tray once more, this time flanked by plates of little sandwiches and cakes. She had handed Lady Manderly her tea and a plate and was offering her the sandwiches when the door opened and Professor Cator came in, and just ahead of him came the girl who had called at the office in Bloomsbury. She was looking more beautiful than ever, in knickerbockers again, this time plaid ones with a fetching little velvet waistcoat and a ridiculous velvet beret perched on her lovely head. She said: 'Hullo, Lady Manderly, I made Alexander bring me here for tea—I'm dying for a cup.' She pecked Lady Manderly's cheek and grinned at Jemima. 'Hullo to you too. Alexander said Lady Manderly had a new companion, though I must say you don't look the part.' She put her head on one side. 'Well, perhaps you do—no glamour, poor dear, and you ought to do something with that mousy hair.'

The Professor had gone to stand by the window after greeting his aunt briefly. He had barely glanced at Jemima, but now he stared at her thoughtfully so that she coloured and frowned. 'I'll ring for more cups,' she said rather primly, and stood by the bell until Belling came into the room. She felt awkward and dreadfully plain, and although the girl hadn't meant to be unkind, her words had poked a hole in Jemima's pride—a hole made much worse by Lady Manderly telling her carelessly to go and have her tea in the room where she had been working that morning. 'Find something to do,' advised Lady Manderly, 'and come back when I ring.'

So Jemima tidied the desk and then sat behind it, longing for her tea and not sure if she was supposed to go in search of it or ring. Probably Belling would object to bringing it to her—after all, she wasn't much better than a servant.

She sat for five minutes or so, getting steadily more and more indignant. She was after all a don's daughter who had enjoyed a social life of sorts, well educated, so that when presently Professor Cator opened the door and came into the room she gave him a look of dislike as well as surprise.

'Ah, you have had no tea,' he observed in a bland voice which made her grit her teeth.

'I don't want any, thank you, Professor Cato,', said Jemima while she thought longingly of a whole teapot full, with sandwiches to go with it.

He took no notice of her at all, but pulled the bell rope and when Belling came, ordered tea to be brought at once. 'And be so good as to put a second cup on the tray,' he finished, and to Jemima's annoyance, sat down.

She could think of nothing to say; she sat behind the desk still, twiddling a pen between her fingers and wishing he would go away.

Something he didn't mean to do, for as the tea tray was borne in and set down on a small table he observed: 'I take milk and two lumps of sugar.'

Jemima raised her eyes to his impassive face. 'Shouldn't you be having tea with Lady Manderly and—and the young lady?'

He shrugged massive shoulders. 'They're discussing some party or other which I found boring.' And at the speaking look she gave him: 'You won't bore me, Miss Mason, because there is no need for us to talk.'

Jemima poured tea carefully from a small silver teapot. 'That's an abominable thing to say,' she pointed out severely, and handed him his cup and saucer. He put it down by his chair and in turn handed her the plate of sandwiches.

It was a little unnerving, but by the time she had given both of them a second cup of tea, and eaten her share of the sandwiches and started upon the really delicious walnut cake, her sensible nature had re-asserted itself. And as for her companion, he appeared to be the picture of ease and contentment, sitting there eating his tea for all the world as if he were alone. It was a chastening thought that she made not the slightest impression upon him, a remark borne out by his: 'You may not set the Thames on fire, Miss Mason, but at least you don't chatter,' as he got to his feet and went out of the room.

She sat very still after he had gone. He had been extremely rude, for two pins she would get her things and leave the house and leave him and his arrogant old aunt to fend for themselves. But of course she couldn't do that; she hadn't two pins, let alone a week's salary, and the beautiful Gloria would undoubtedly fend very nicely for the Professor.

She heard their voices presently as they prepared to leave, and shortly afterwards Lady Manderly swept into the room, told her to get the tray taken away, and when that was done, began on a list of names of those who were to be invited to a party she intended giving. 'In two weeks' time,' she observed. 'Just a small affair—my birthday, you know.' She shot a glance at Jemima. 'There will be a good deal of organising to do.'

From which Jemima concluded that she was to be organiser in chief.

Lady Manderly was still murmuring on about smoked salmon and should she have oyster patties when the carriage clock above the fireplace tinkled the hour. Jemima finished the note she was making and closed the book.

'I'll start on the invitations tomorrow morning, shall I, Lady Manderly?' She stood up, aware that Lady Manderly was looking surprised. 'It's six o'clock,' she went on.

Lady Manderly snapped: 'A clockwatcher, are you? Another half hour or so . . .'

'I'm sorry, but it's quite a long day, you know, and I have things to do in the evenings—besides, you wouldn't want to pay me overtime, Lady Manderly.'

Her employer gobbled. 'Overtime? I have no intention of paying you overtime!'

'No, I didn't think you would want to, that's why I'm going now. Good evening, Lady Manderly.'

Jemima smiled kindly at her companion, who was obviously struggling for words, but by the time she had decided what to say, Jemima had gone.

The flat, when she reached it, looked small and poky and her room dark and shabby, but she told herself that that was because she had just come from such luxurious surroundings. She tidied herself and in response to Shirley's cheerful shout, went along to the sitting room and sat down to the supper they had invited her to share. Mrs Adams and Shirley greeted her with a casual friendliness which was heartwarming after the arrogance of her employer and Professor Cator's indifference and rudeness. They piled her plate high with food, poured strong tea and plied her with questions.

'What's the old lady like?' asked Shirley eagerly, and before Jemima could answer: 'What's the house like inside?' asked her mother.

'Very large,' said Jemima, and thought that answered both questions very adequately, but it wouldn't do to make fun of her employer. 'Lots of lovely furniture and thick velvet curtains. I haven't seen any bedrooms, indeed I've only been in three rooms; the drawing-room is magnificent, a bit like a museum, you know. I work in a smaller room with just a desk and a table and chair or two, and we had lunch in a dining room at the back of the house . . .'

'And the old lady?'

'Very—very dignified. Tall and stout and beautifully dressed. There's a butler and I suppose there are maids as well, though I haven't seen any yet.'

'What did you eat?' asked Mrs Adams, and cast an involuntary glance at the remains of the steak and kidney pudding on the plastic tablecloth.

'Well, it sounds a lot, but it wasn't nearly as good as this pudding, Mrs Adams. It was awfully kind of you to ask me to share it . . .'

'It's your first day,' explained Mrs Adams. 'Well, what did you eat?'

'Soup—just a little bowl full—a clear soup.'

Shirley sniffed. 'Bovril watered down!'

'And then a fish soufflé with spinach and afterwards a creme caramel.'

'Not enough to put into a hollow tooth, I'll be bound. Tell you what, love, you can eat with us in the evenings for another two pounds a week. Shan't make anything out of it, but it's just as easy to cook for three as two and it'll give you a bit more time to enjoy yourself.' Mrs Adams added sharply: 'There ain't no butler, mind, nor no pudding for afters. Just a cup of tea.'

'You're very kind, Mrs Adams, and I'd love to do that if you're sure it doesn't put you out. Only if you have visitors will you say so and I'll have supper in my room? It'll be lovely to come back to a meal in the evenings, it seemed a long day, but I daresay once I know more about the work, the days will go faster.'

Shirley gave her a look of sympathy tinged with pity. 'Sounds like a dull old job to me,' she observed. 'Any men around?'

'There's Belling the butler, but he's elderly and a bit severe . . .' She hesitated and Shirley said quickly: 'And someone else?'

'He doesn't really count,' said Jemima slowly. 'He's

Lady Manderly's nephew—a Professor of Endocrinology, but he doesn't live there. He came this afternoon with a girl, an absolutely gorgeous creature. You
know, golden hair and blue eyes and most wonderful
clothes—those knickerbockers, and a waistcoat and the
most heavenly boots.'

'Got 'im 'ooked, 'as she?' Mrs Adams wanted to
know. 'I don't 'old with them knickers, nor don't
Shirley's young man.'

Shirley pouted. 'Old-fashioned, that's what 'e is,' she
complained, 'always talking about moons and roses and
Ginger Rogers dresses!'

'Well, they were rather fetching,' said Jemima, and
far safer for Shirley, she thought privately; such a nice
friendly girl, but her legs didn't bear too much lime-
light on them. Nor do mine, for that matter, thought
Jemima, erroneously, as a matter of fact; she had nice
legs, but since no one had ever told her so, she took it
for granted that they were better concealed by a skirt.

She helped with the washing up presently and then
went to her room to write to Dick before making herself a mug of cocoa on the gas ring. She lit the gas fire,
and sitting up in bed, reading, belatedly, the morning
paper, she decided that the little room wasn't too bad
at all. Tomorrow she would buy some flowers, she
promised herself, and in a week or two, when she had
a little money to spare, she would buy one of those
cheerful coloured rugs and a cushion or two. She didn't
allow herself to think about her old home; it had gone
for good, and she had been lucky to find someone as
kind as Mrs Adams. She turned out the fire and the
light and closed her eyes. She had a job too, although
she wondered sleepily just how long she would keep it.
Lady Manderly was an old tyrant and Jemima, although tolerant to a fault, had no intention of being

anyone's doormat. She would see how the cat jumped, but meanwhile, she told herself resolutely, she was both happy and content. Not quite, perhaps; no girl, however happy and content, liked to be told that she wouldn't set the Thames on fire. 'Beastly man,' said Jemima aloud, and went to sleep.

It was all go the next day. Lady Manderly, disappointed that Jemima should present herself exactly at nine o'clock, was inclined to be tetchy and had to content herself with the remark that she hoped that Jemima would continue to be punctual each morning. 'As punctual as you were leaving yesterday evening,' she added sourly.

Jemima agreed with her cheerfully and began sorting the post. She followed yesterday's pattern exactly so that beyond a frustrated snort from her employer, nothing had to be said. It was fortunate that the paper reported at great length the wedding of a peer of the realm's daughter. Jemima prudently earmarked it for reading, discarded the more gloomy titbits, studied the weather forecast, found an amusing story about a dog purported to play the piano, and held herself ready to receive Lady Manderly's instructions.

There were a great many of them, and they kept Jemima occupied for the rest of the morning, so that, by the time they had had lunch and she had taken Coco for a long-delayed walk, it was time for the tea tray to be brought in, and since there was no Professor and no Gloria today, she was able to drink her tea in comparative peace, if she discounted Lady Manderly's frequent demands for this that and the other to be done at once.

She left the house promptly, shared a supper of toad-in-the-hole with Shirley and her mother and then, unable to bear her little room after the spaciousness of

Lady Manderly's house, went for a walk. It was a cool evening and she walked fast, not noticing where she went and when she got back to her little room she was tired enough to go straight to bed and sleep, which was a good thing, for she was feeling utterly miserable.

But with the morning she felt better. Here she was half way through the week, and pay day within sight too. She presented a calm face towards Lady Manderly, carried out her manifold duties and went back to the flat that evening feeling that at least she was holding her own. And for the next couple of days she was busy enough not to have the time to mope, indeed she was surprised to find that she was actually beginning to enjoy herself. True, Lady Manderly never ceased to remind her that she had no qualifications of any sort and that a girl in her position should be able to type at the very least, but on the other hand, she was forced to concede that Jemima had a pleasant voice, good manners and didn't answer back. On the whole, they were beginning to like each other, in a guarded way.

It was raining when Jemima left for work the next morning, with a mean little wind which hinted of winter ahead. She skimmed along into its teeth and was almost at the house when a car, driven too fast, forced her against the railings, checked momentarily, and then drove off.

Jemima looked at her mud-spattered legs. 'The horrible wretch!' she muttered with a good deal of feeling, and then repeated herself at the sight of the furry heap in the middle of the road. It mewed soundlessly and stared at her with beseaching eyes, and she went to it at once, kneeling down in the muddy road to touch it with a gentle hand. 'Oh, my poor dear!' She was so angry and upset she could hardly get the words out.

'That devil! Let me take a look.'

The little beast lay still as she felt it carefully through its sodden fur, but it bared its teeth as she touched its hind legs. She would have to get it to a vet as quickly as possible. She stroked its head while she thought what was best to be done. Lady Manderly's house was only a few doors away, she could at least telephone from there, but the thought of leaving the little cat in the road made her hesitate. If only someone would come . . .

She barely heard the car purring to a halt, but she looked round when the car door was slammed and someone came towards her. Professor Cator. She wasted no time. 'Oh, good, I'm glad it's you,' she told him urgently. 'Some fiend ran over this poor little beast not five minutes ago and didn't stop. I think he's broken his back legs, but I'm not sure. Would you mind telephoning a vet for me, I can't leave him here.'

The Professor didn't say anything, only crouched down beside her and looked closely at the animal. 'Go and get into the car,' he told her. 'I'll bring him over to you, he can lie on your lap—it'll be much easier to take him to a vet straight away.'

She hesitated. 'Yes, but won't you hurt him?'

He said dryly: 'Not intentionally, Miss Mason, and he can't stay here.'

Jemima did as she was told then, getting into the front seat and leaving the door open. A Rolls-Royce, she noticed vaguely, gleaming and spotless and the acme of comfort. She sat with her head averted because she couldn't bear to see how the Professor would manage, but in no time at all the little cat was on her knee and he was sitting beside her, reversing the big car and driving back the way he had came.

'Is there a vet close by?' she asked.

'I've no idea, I'm taking him to my own vet.' The tone of his voice didn't encourage her to talk; she sat without speaking until he turned down a narrow street and pulled up before a small door in a high wall. 'Wait here,' he told her, and got out and went through the door, to return very shortly with a short thin man who nodded at her, eased the cat on to what looked like a miniature stretcher, and went back through the door. The Professor went with him and she was left sitting there, suddenly in a frightful state because she had remembered that she should have been at her desk all of twenty minutes ago. Probably she would get the sack, she thought unhappily, in which case was she entitled to a week's salary? Or was she entitled to no salary at all?

When, after another five minutes, Professor Cator returned she turned to him with a worried face. 'I'm so late . . .' and then, because the little cat was really more important: 'Can the vet do something? Will it be all right?'

The Professor got in beside her. 'Yes, he'll set the legs and look after the little beast until it's fit to go to whoever will have it.' He gave her a sideways look as he spoke. 'You?' he asked blandly.

She said at once: 'Yes, of course. The fees . . .?'

'The vet never charges for this kind of accident.' He watched the relief on her face with detached amusement. 'I telephoned my aunt and explained why you would be late.'

He was driving back the way they had come, showing no further interest in her.

'Oh, did you? How kind—I was a bit worried. I mean, Lady Manderly likes me to be punctual, and I thought . . . that is, I was afraid she might have given me the sack.'

He said casually: 'Yes, I was surprised she was so forbearing. You'll only be half an hour or so late, though.'

'Yes, and I can make it up this evening.'

'You live close by?'

'Yes, quite a short walk.' She had no intention of telling him where. The little newspaper shop was hardly a good address; even as she thought it she felt mean. Mrs Adams and Shirley were kind and friendly and however poky her room was, it was her own while she paid the rent. 'I'm very comfortable at the flat,' she told him with a shade of defiance and a regrettable lack of truth, and was sorry she had said it, because he didn't show any interest. She doubted if he was listening; he was probably bored stiff by the whole little episode.

She was left to face Lady Manderly alone. The Professor gave her a curt nod when they reached the house, leaned over and opened the door for her and drove off without a second glance.

'Rather rude,' muttered Jemima, and thumped the door knocker with unnecessary violence.

Belling admitted her and allowed a faint sympathetic smile to crease his bland features. 'Lady Manderly is in the small sitting room, miss, if you would go up at once.'

Lady Manderly, empurpled with ill humour, received her coldly. 'It is to be hoped,' she uttered sternly, 'that you will not make a habit of rescuing animals when you should be here working for me.'

'It's to be hoped that there won't be any more animals to rescue,' observed Jemima reasonably. 'I'm sorry I'm late, Lady Manderly, but I couldn't have left that cat lying there in the middle of the road . . .'

Her employer raised a majestic hand. 'Spare me the

details, Miss Mason, I do not wish to hear them.'

'That's the trouble, isn't it?' said Jemima equably. 'People never want to hear about misery and pain, do they?'

Lady Manderly drew in a hissing breath, lifted her lorgnette and stared at Jemima through them, and then flung them back on to her generous front so fiercely that the chain snapped and the whole lot fell on to the carpet.

'There, now see what you've done,' said Jemima chidingly. 'I told you that specs would be easier for you.' She got down on her knees and picked up the broken chain. 'I'll get some thread and tie the links together until we can get it mended.'

Lady Manderly was opening and closing her mouth like a dying fish, struggling to get out words. At last she managed: 'You are a forward girl . . .'

'I don't mean to be,' said Jemima, and smiled nicely at the cross face.

'Would you like me to read to you first this morning, there don't seem to be many letters.' She glanced at the unopened pile on the desk.

'Very well,' said Lady Manderly ungraciously, and then: 'Really, I don't know if you will suit, Miss Mason.'

Jemima's heart sank, but she turned a calm face to her employer.

'Would you like me to draft another advertisement?' she asked matter-of-factly.

Lady Manderly bristled. 'You don't like your work here? You wish to leave?'

'Me? Heavens, no! I'm very happy, you see I had an invalid mother to look after for a few years and I—I miss caring for someone.'

Lady Manderly's rather protuberant eyes popped

out still further and for once she had no answer. Jemima hadn't expected one, she skimmed through the news, picking out the choicest bits. 'Shall I start reading, Lady Manderly?' she asked.

'Yes, you may do so, Miss Mason. You say that you are happy here—that being so, I am prepared to over- look your lateness this morning. After all, my nephew seems to think that you are a good enough young woman.'

'How very kind of him,' said Jemima softly and her fine eyes sparkled with temper at the arrogance of it.

'So you will stay?' asked Lady Manderly, and Jemima detected the tiniest hint of wistfulness in the commanding voice.

'Yes, I'd like to, Lady Manderly.' She smiled at the lady and picked up the paper. 'There is a report on the P.M.'s speech—shall I read it to you first?'

The morning went as usual after that, and at lunch time, Lady Manderly made gracious conversation, presumably offering an olive branch of sorts. Jemima was a good listener; they rose from the table in charity with each other and Jemima, having seen Lady Manderly safely tucked up in the drawing room, whisked herself out of the house with Coco, just as eager for a walk as she was.

It was almost six o'clock, and Jemima was just finishing the last of the letters when the phone rang.

'You leave at five o'clock, do you not?' asked the Professor into her ear.

'No, I don't, Professor.' Remembering that he had called her a good enough young woman, she asked in a freezing voice: 'You wish to speak to Lady Manderly?'

'No, not particularly, I thought you might like to know that the little cat is recovering nicely. Have you attempted to find out if it belongs to anyone?'

'How could I do that?' she asked with a snap. 'I've had no time at all. I'll go round to every house this evening when I'm free to do so.'

'If you hadn't taken me up so sharply, I would have continued,' said the Professor mildly. 'The cat is obviously a stray, ill cared for and half starved. If I might suggest—without my head being bitten off—that she remains with the vet until she is quite well, then if you wish to have her you can do so, if not, we must find a good home for her.'

'Oh, yes—well, that would be nice, but the vet won't keep her for nothing? Will he? Could I have his phone number or his name—the bill, you know.'

'I thought I had made myself clear already, Miss Mason. He doesn't charge for emergency treatment, and I will settle the account . . .'

Jemima said suddenly: 'You're an endocrinologist, aren't you? Belling told me. Do you use cats to—to experiment on? Because if that's the reason . . .'

His voice cut through hers like cold steel. 'Miss Mason, I do not, as you put it, use cats. I never have done nor do I intend to, but since you are determined to think the worst of me I suggest we end our conversation.'

He hung up before she could so much as draw breath.

She licked down the last envelope, wondering if she had hurt his feelings—or was he a man with feelings to hurt? Just his pride perhaps. In any case she would have to apologise. She picked up the letters to post and went along to the drawing room to wish Lady Manderly goodnight and went slowly out of the house and down the street.

'Bother the man,' she muttered, 'I hope I never see him again!' The thought was a little lowering for some reason; she brightened visibly when she remembered that she would have to in order to apologise.

CHAPTER THREE

JEMIMA didn't see him for a whole week; although he did in fact leave a message with Belling on two occasions, letting her know that the little cat was making progress. And when she did see him again, he had Gloria with him; they arrived one early afternoon just as Jemima was about to take Coco for her walk. Gloria was wearing a dashing tartan outfit with long leather boots which must have cost the earth. She had a fetching, slightly ridiculous hat perched on her lovely head and wore the smug expression of one who knows she looks as near perfection as possible. As well she might, conceded Jemima sourly, aware of her own shortcomings.

Gloria grinned at her and waved an airy hand. 'Hullo there, how's a life of toil suiting you, darling?' She eyed her with a faintly malicious smile. 'You could do with a visit to the hairdresser, if you don't mind my saying so.'

Jemima bent to fasten Coco's lead on to the silly jewel-studded collar. Words, heated words, jostled on her tongue, but she had no intention of allowing them to be uttered. She was rather red in the face as she straightened up, but she managed a smile.

'No time,' she said with false cheerfulness, and made for the street door. The Professor was standing just inside it, apparently wrapped in thought, and she went past him without looking at him. It was a surprise therefore when he opened it for her and joined her on the pavement.

'The little cat is well enough to leave the vet,' he told her blandly. 'I'll fetch her this evening and bring her to your flat.'

Jemima stood staring up at him, unaware of the horror on her face. He saw it and wondered with a faint spark of interest why it was there.

'Oh, well,' she said in a rush, 'I—I haven't told my landlady—she might not . . . that is . . .'

'I should anticipate no difficulty, Miss Mason, unless you live in a council flat.'

'No, no, I don't.'

'Then there should be nothing to worry you.' He waited a bit to see if she was going to tell him what the difficulty was, but when she didn't speak: 'I will meet you here at six o'clock.'

Jemima sought feverishly for an excuse and could think of none—not that it mattered; he had turned on his heel and gone back into the house before she had got her addled wits working.

She spent the rest of the afternoon examining various wholly unsatisfactory ways of getting out of the mess, and rejecting them in turn, to the detriment of her work, so that Lady Manderly had the satisfaction of calling her to order several times.

Six o'clock came too soon, and when she suggested that she should stay a little while and check the grocery bills due to be paid, she was told quite sharply to go home at once. She took as long as she could to leave the house, going back twice on trumped-up excuses, but in the end, almost fifteen minutes late, she had to open the door, buoyed up with the very faint hope that the Professor had got sick of waiting for her.

He hadn't. There was the Rolls, parked opposite with him at the wheel. He leaned over and opened the door as she went reluctantly across the pavement and observed drily: 'I'm still here, you see. Get in. Where do you live?'

She saw a possible loophole of escape and said quickly: 'Oh, quite close by. If you'd just let me have the cat, I can walk there . . .'

For answer he started the car and swung it round. 'The address?' he persisted in a voice which would brook no denial.

He made no comment as he stopped the car in front of Mrs Adams' shop. It was still open, although there were no customers there. Shirley was starting to tidy away the racks of magazines and comics, and she glanced up as Jemima got out of the car and crossed the pavement.

'Cor, look who's 'ere, come 'ome in a posh car!' She caught sight of the Professor straightening his splendid person to his full height, cat basket in hand, and her eyes almost started from her head. 'And Prince Charming tagging along, an' all.' She grinned widely at Jemima. 'Oo's yer posh friend, Jemima?'

Jemima had gone a little pink, but she said clearly: 'Shirley, this is Professor Cator, who has most kindly given me a lift back.' She gave him a fleeting look. 'Professor, this is Miss Shirley Adams.'

He took the hand offered him and shook it firmly. 'I'll come up with you, if I may, Miss Mason?' He looked enquiringly at Shirley as he spoke and she flung the door at the back of the shop open. 'Go ahead,' she begged him, and winked at Jemima.

There was nothing for it but to climb the shabby stairs with him hard on her heels. As they reached the landing the smell of frying fish was heavy on the air, a sign that Mrs Adams was in the kitchen, fortunately with the door shut. Jemima breathed a small sigh of relief and led the way down the passage and opened her door.

'It isn't a flat,' she told him forthrightly. 'I should have told you that in the first place, shouldn't I?'

He closed the door behind him. 'Yes, you should,' and then surprisingly he added in a quite gentle voice, 'But I quite see why you didn't.' He smiled at her so kindly that she smiled too, a little uncertainly, and he went on: 'Of course you can't keep a cat here; she shall come home with me.'

He put the basket down on the bed and stood in the middle of the room, towering over everything, and since Jemima had nothing to say to that, he bent and let the cat out and tucked her under his arm. 'Perhaps I might sit down?' he suggested softly.

Jemima's face, until now pale with fright, coloured fiercely. 'I'm so sorry, please do—not the chair, though, it's not very strong. Perhaps the bed, if you wouldn't mind.'

He sat down beside the little cat and scooped her on to his knee. Its hind legs were in plaster, but its coat was soft and shining and its small face was nicely plump.

Jemima tickled her chin with a gentle finger. 'I wish I could have her—she's beautiful, isn't she? Will her legs be all right?'

'The vet says so. Tell me, Jemima, how much does my aunt pay you each week?'

'Fifty pounds, and I have my lunch and tea at her house.'

'And the rent here?'

It really wasn't his business, but somehow she found herself answering him. 'Forty pounds a week, but I get a good breakfast and my supper as well as this room.'

'No extras?' he asked casually.

'Well, this fire, and the gas ring—there's a meter, and ten pence a day for a bath, but I haven't any fares. I have plenty to live on, Professor Cator.'

'But not much to spend.'

'Enough. Lady Manderly likes me to have lunch with her on my half day, so I don't get back here much before two o'clock, and by the time I've done what shopping I need to do, it's tea time. And on Sundays I go to church and explore London. I don't know it very well.'

'You have friends?'

She could have lied about that, but his rather hard grey eyes were on her face. 'Oh, yes, but they all live in Oxford—that is—that was—my home.'

'Ah yes, my aunt mentioned that.' He wasn't looking at her, but stroking the cat curled up on his knee. 'If you wish I could find you somewhere more suitable in which to live.'

She looked like an eager child. 'Oh, could you? That would be . . . no, it wouldn't do. I can't leave here, not yet. You see, Mrs Adams and Shirley were very kind to me—I had nowhere to go, and they offered me a room . . .' She paused and looked at him, remote, polite and probably bored to death. 'I don't suppose you've ever found yourself without a home?' she observed. 'It's not pleasant.' There was no trace of self-pity in her quiet voice.

'I imagine not.' He put the cat back into the basket and stood up. 'You must do as you wish, Jemima.'

She went to open the door. 'I'm very grateful for the offer, Professor Cator, and for your kindness in taking the little cat. I'm sorry I misled you.'

He said austerely: 'Yes, don't do it again, but I think perhaps that you will not—it would be quite useless, you know.'

The kitchen door was open now and a blue haze redolent of fish hung over the landing. Mrs Adams stood there, obviously primed by Shirley and anxious to see their visitor. She looked a little belligerent, for she didn't hold with gentlemen followers to girls living in bedsitters, but as her eye lighted upon the Professor her expression changed. Here was a gent all right, lovely manners too—coming straight to her and shaking her hand and saying how delighted his aunt was that Miss Mason had found such a comfortable room and such a kind landlady.

'Well, I'm sure I do me best,' said Mrs Adams, much gratified. 'Such a nice young lady too—me and Shirl saw that first go off—we're glad ter 'ave her.'

She melted visibly under Professor Cator's charm, and Jemima, watching, saw that he could be very charming indeed if he wanted to. He shook Mrs Adams hand. 'I'll leave you to your supper,' he said pleasantly, and bade her good evening. With Jemima ahead of him he went downstairs and into the shop where Shirley was still pottering about, although the closed sign was on the door now. ' 'Ad a nice chat?' she asked brightly, and unlocked the door. The Professor gave her a pleasant smile, nodded briskly to Jemima, then got back into his car and drove away.

'What's in the basket?' asked Shirley as they stood watching the Rolls' imposing back disappear.

'A cat. He rescued it and took it to a vet to be cured. He's taking it to his home.'

'Where's he live?'

'I've no idea.'

'Well, if I was you, I'd jolly well find out. He's a bit

of all right—'andsome and loaded. I fancy 'im.' She shot a look at Jemima. 'Don't you?'

Jemima was going upstairs. 'No—no, I don't. You see, I don't know anything about him. Besides, he's got a smashing blonde.'

'What's that got to do with it?' asked Shirley.

Jemima turned round to look at her. 'Everything in the world. She's the loveliest girl I've ever seen, Shirley, and she wears clothes straight out of *Harpers*.'

They were on the landing and Jemima turned away to go to her room. 'I must just tidy myself,' she added.

'Well, and she may be a raving beauty,' said Shirley, 'but you've got class, Jemima—stands out a mile, it does—she'll loose 'er looks by the time she's thirty, and you'll be just like you are now.'

'Thanks, Shirley.' Jemima gave a chuckle. 'But I've not got long to go—I'm twenty-seven, as near as not.'

She was kept busy for the next few days; the replies to the invitations she had sent out were coming in fast and Lady Manderly was enjoying herself giving orders and then countermanding them, changing the refreshments almost hourly, sending back the dress she was to wear, arguing with the caterers. And all of it done through Jemima, who spent hours on the phone placating the irate people at the other end.

'You will, of course, remain here on the evening of the party,' said Lady Manderly. 'I shall need someone to see that everything goes smoothly. You may have your supper here,' she added graciously I'll tell Belling to see that a tray is taken to the small sitting room for you. I don't expect you to meet any of my guests.'

Jemima's eyes sparkled with rage, she said gently: 'Well, that's a good thing, because I don't believe I would wish to meet them,' she ignored Lady Manderly's outraged look and went on opening the letters. 'There are three guests who can't come,' she pointed out. 'Would you like me to send invitations to replace them?' She handed them over to her employer, still dangerously plum-coloured, and picked up the list of guests from the desk. 'There are several names you queried.'

The list was taken from her. 'You may take Coco for her walk,' said Lady Manderly, 'I'll decide while you are gone. Be back in an hour's time.'

And for once Jemima was only too glad to be back in an hour; Lady Manderly had entirely overlooked the fact that it was drizzling with rain. She handed Coco, damp despite her tartan jacket, over to Belling and peeled off her own wet mackintosh.

'It's foul outside, Belling,' she said cheerfully. 'I used to like October in Oxford, but I don't like it here—all wet pavements and umbrellas.'

'There is a nice fire in Cook's room, miss, if you could spare a minute.' Belling gave her a fatherly look, 'and I daresay a nice cup of tea.'

'Oh, Belling, you are kind, but I'd better go straight up—there's an awful lot to do, only do ask me again when I'm not busy, it sounds lovely.'

Belling watched her fly upstairs and went back to the kitchen with Coco. 'That's a nice young lady,' he confided to Cook. 'You don't meet her sort these days. I only hope she stays with us.'

Cook nodded her head. 'You're right, Mr Belling, she's worth a dozen of that young madam who's always in and out with Professor Cator. Nothing between the ears,' she added tartly.

'Ah, but she's got looks, and our young lady hasn't,' declared Mr Belling sagely, 'and it's looks that count with the gentlemen.'

'And I'll be so bold as to question that, Mr Belling

The Professor's no fool, else he'd have married years ago. I've lost count of the pretty girls he's brought here.'

Long before the first guest arrived, Jemima was worn out. She was a strong girl despite her small stature, but Lady Manderly was difficult, her forceful nature not in the least softened by the fact that it was her birthday, and she had spent the day finding fault with everything and everyone. Jemima had a number of cards to open and hand on to her and innumerable small parcels, but Lady Manderly had very little to say about any of them. Viewing a knitted shawl with dislike, she observed tartly: 'Twice a year I am plagued, at Christmas and my birthday—they hope to be remembered in my will, of course.'

Jemima, who had debated whether to send her employer a card, was thankful that she had decided against it.

The guests had been invited for nine o'clock; there was to be general conversation—or so Lady Manderly had decreed—dancing, and at eleven o'clock a buffet supper.

Jemima was to stay until the last guest had gone in to supper and then was free to go home, something would be brought to her on a tray during the course of the evening, once the dancing had started.

Jemima, hearing this, had suggested that she might go back to her room and have her supper and return in good time before the first guest appeared, but Lady Manderly would have none of it; the idea was vetoed at once and in no uncertain terms, so there was nothing for it but to eat as much as she could at tea and hope that the dancing would start as soon as possible.

But as it turned out she had no time at all even to sneak a sandwich from the plates standing ready in the kitchen. Lady Manderly had taken strong exception to a floral arrangement in the drawing room which Jemima was ordered to rearrange at once, and then when the small band arrived it was discovered that the guitarist was in no fit state to perform. There was no time to get anyone to take his place. Jemima got him down to the kitchen where she plied him with hot black coffee until she was called away once more to another small crisis—one of the hired waiters had dropped a bowl of trifle. Jemima didn't waste time looking at the mess. She suggested calmly that it should be bundled up in a newspaper and taken at once to a dustbin, out of sight, and that the floor should be cleaned just as soon as possible. The chance of Lady Manderly coming into the kitchen was remote, but that lady was unpredictable; if she chose to visit her domestic quarters in purple satin and diamonds, she would do so without warning.

'Will someone get me a big bowl,' asked Jemima urgently, and stuck her neat head into the freezer. She addressed Cook, busy with canapés on the other side of the kitchen. 'Mrs Betts, do you mind if I stay here for a minute and see if we can concoct something to look like a trifle?'

Mrs Betts dipped a very careful knife into caviare. 'You go ahead, Miss Mason, take what you want.' She glanced up briefly and smiled; a nice calm young lady, she thought, such a pity she wasn't pretty.

Something looking like the ornate trifle which had been dropped began to take shape under Jemima's hands. With a final topping of whipped cream, a sprinkling of glacé cherries and a nut or two, it looked moderately like the genuine article, although its inside—ice cream sponge cake, a couple of tins of fruit and a liberal dash of the cooking sherry in the cupboard—was going to taste different. 'For heaven's sake,' Jemima told Belling, 'see that this one's kept well away from Lady Manderly!'

She was washing her hands at the sink when one of the maids came hurrying in. 'My lady wants you at once, miss, she's in her bedroom.'

Jemima hadn't been there before. It was a vast, high ceilinged room, furnished with enormous pieces in mahogany; the windows were draped in velvet with heavy pelmets and the bed had a matching velvet canopy. In the middle of this splendour stood Lady Manderly, upholstered in the purple satin and diamonds Jemima had been told about but had not yet seen. She presented an overwhelmingly impressive sight. Jemima gulped. 'That's a very handsome gown, Lady Manderly. You'll be the centre of attraction.'

'So I should be,' said Lady Manderly sharply. 'It's my birthday party. Now go downstairs like a good girl and be sure to let me know the instant the first car stops in front of the door.'

Jemima went back down the staircase, wondering why Lady Manderly wasn't going down to the drawing-room on the first floor to receive her guests, but there wasn't much time to ponder the matter. Belling had taken up position in the hall and two of the maids hovered ready to lead the ladies above to the bedrooms allotted for their prinking. A moment later headlights swept to a standstill before the door and then a second car behind them. Jemima whisked up the stairs again.

'Wait until I've greeted my guests,' commanded Lady Manderly, 'and then go along to the bedrooms set aside for the ladies and make sure that they have everything they require.'

She sailed off, and Jemima muttered a naughty word under her breath and crossed the landing. Half way there she heard Lady Manderly's voice: 'My dears, I should be in the drawing-room, but there's been so much to attend to and really no one capable of doing the smallest thing right.'

There was a murmur from the staircase. The ladies would be arriving on the landing at any moment. Jemima, composing a letter of resignation in her mind, switched on all the lights, gave the three ladies a civil good evening and went down the back stairs to the kitchen. It might be Lady Manderly's birthday, but that was no reason to belittle everyone around her. She hadn't lifted a single beringed finger to aid those who had toiled to make the party a success and Jemima for one was going to say so. She flounced into the kitchen, her placid face so thunderous that Cook made haste to pour her a cup of coffee before accepting her help in arranging vol-au-vents on a number of silver dishes.

'Been at you?' she asked sympathetically. 'Don't you take no notice, Miss Jemima. Born selfish, she was, and she'll die the same way. 'Er own family find her a trial, I can tell you, you must be the sixth or seventh companion they've advertised for. 'Er own children keep well away, I can tell you—if it wasn't for Professor Cator, no one would go near 'er.'

Jemima swallowed her coffee and began on the vol-au-vents. She said politely: 'Really?'

'Yes—it's 'im 'oo advertises for the companions and takes a quick look at 'em first. We none of us thought you'd do, but I must say you've got a way with you. That'll be you living at Oxford,' she finished ingenuously. She added to make it quite clear: 'Educated, aren't you? Some of the others weren't—didn't know 'ow to go with folk.' She accepted a dish from Jemima. 'I'm sure we all 'opes that you'll stay, Miss Jemima.'

Which, seeing that Jemima had made up her mind

to go, was a bit unsettling.

Guests were arriving thick and fast. Jemima, leaping around from kitchen to bedroom, had time to do no more than glimpse them as she supplied pins and combs and hair sprays, wondering as she did so why so many of the women arrived lacking these small necessities.

'And who are you, my dear?' asked one elderly lady as Jemima pinned the hem of her gown. But before she could answer a thin young woman with a cross face said sharply: 'She's Lady Manderly's paid companion. She must be at least the sixth in the last year.' Her cold eyes surveyed Jemima. 'And from the look of her, there'll be a new one in no time at all.'

Just as though I'm not here, thought Jemima, and pinned the rest of the hem any old how, then turning a deaf ear to the thin woman's cries for aspirin, she went out of the room, shutting the door behind her. As far as she was concerned the evening was not being a success.

It seemed a very long time before the guests were all safely in the vast drawing-room. Jemima arranged the mountains of fur coats tidily so that their owners could find them easily and went hopefully to the small sitting-room. Cook and Belling had done her proud. A tray had been arranged on the desk—soup, fragrant in a covered pipkin, a plate of dainties; smoked salmon, some of the vol-au-vents she had helped prepare, pâté and hot toast, lobster patties, a salade Niçoise and some strawberry tartlets topped with whipped cream, and by way of accompanying these delicacies, there was a glass of white wine and a thermos jug of coffee.

Jemima sat down at the desk and took a sip of the wine. She was tired and cross, but her supper was such a pleasant surprise that she was beginning to feel better already. She had the soup, the pâté and toast and was

about to start off on the lobster patties when she caught
sight of the *Daily Telegraph* on the table by the
window. She found a pen, turned to the crossword and
started on it between mouthfuls of patty. That left the
smoked salmon and salad. She finished the wine and
began on the salmon. It was getting on for eleven
o'clock; she would be able to go home very shortly
now. Everything was going well. She had taken a look
at the dining-room, spread with the buffet supper, and
agreed with Belling that it looked splendid and the
birthday cake was a masterpiece. She had popped down
to the kitchen to see if anyone needed a hand, and
found them taking their supper in relays; no ladies had
needed pinning up or calming down. She finished the
salmon and attacked the tarts.

She was lifting the first one to her mouth when the
door opened and Professor Cator came in. Jemima, her
mouth slightly open to receive the tart, stared at him
over its mound of cream.

He stood for a moment looking back at her and then sat
down on the arm of the chair his aunt invariably sat in.

'Why aren't you downstairs with the guests?' he
wanted to know.

Jemima took a defiant bite. From a slightly full mouth
she said: 'I'm not a guest, that's why.'

'An error on the part of my aunt, for which I apologise. You have organised it all very well.'

She licked a crumb away with the tip of her tongue.
'Well, I've done it before, you know, at home,' she
said ungraciously. 'You don't mind if I finish my
supper? I may go home at eleven o'clock.'

His cold eyes flickered over the almost empty tray.
'I hope Belling saw that you had sufficient of everything.'

'Oh, he did, thank you.' She poured a cup of coffee

and took an appreciative sip and eyed the remaining tarts.

'I should finish them,' suggested the Professor blandly. 'Tell me, are you being paid for these extra hours?'

'I don't know, but I should imagine not. Companions don't have regular hours.' She remembered the thin young woman's remarks about paid companions and frowned heavily. 'I intend to give in my notice tomorrow,' she told him.

He was much too discerning. 'Because of something someone said? Or has my aunt been worse than usual?'

Jemima bit into the last tart. 'Both.'

'You have another job in view?'

'No.'

'I have been talking to my aunt this evening and suggested that she should stay for a while at her house in Stratford-on-Avon. Do you know the town?'

'Very well—we used to go over to the Royal Shakespeare Theatre regularly.'

'My aunt has a house on the outskirts of the town; she has a number of acquaintances living in the area, you would have a good deal more time to yourself. You would have to live there, of course.' He gave her a long hard look. 'You look as though you could do with a holiday.'

Jemima put down her coffee cup. 'How long for?'

He shrugged his shoulders. 'A month, six weeks. If at the end of that time you still feel you must leave, it would be easier to make the break before returning here, wouldn't it?' He added thoughtfully: 'You would be near enough to Oxford to spend some time with your friends there.'

'I had decided to leave.'

'Yes, I know, but would you stay, as a favour to me?'

She opened her lovely eyes wide. 'Why on earth should I do you a favour?' and then, 'Oh, because you gave a home to the little cat . . .'

'No, that hadn't entered my head. It may surprise you to know that I'm quite fond of my aunt; you are the only girl so far who has come to terms with her. All the others either grovelled or were pert. You merely speak your mind in such a reasonable manner that she accepts it. And don't look at me like that—she has told me this herself.'

Jemima poured herself a second cup of coffee. There was no reason at all why she should oblige the Professor; he had never been particularly nice to her, although he had been kindness itself towards the little cat, and there was no getting away from the fact that Lady Manderly was a difficult employer. On the other hand, she needed to earn her living and if possible save a little money; enough to keep her while she took a course of shorthand and typing, or found a shop job, and that wouldn't be easy. She wasn't the type of girl to work in a boutique or fashionable dress shop, she wasn't pretty or smart enough; she liked books, but she had a vague idea that one needed to have some kind of a diploma before getting a job as a librarian or in a decent bookshop. It would have to be something dull like stationery or groceries . . .

'Well?' asked Professor Cator impatiently. 'You're taking a long time to make up your mind. If it's money you are worrying about, your salary will be the same, so it will cost you nothing for lodgings. You'll be able to save some money.'

She gave him a cold look. He had a nasty way of stating facts too baldly. She doubted if his lovely Gloria had ever been spoken to like that, and what exactly did he mean? Was she to save for her old age, or because no one would want to marry her? If she saved any money at all, she would spend every farthing on something quite unsuitable, like a holiday in the South of France, or a complete outfit from Harrods—there had been a skirt and blouse and matching jacket in the window—a rich, very expensive green . . .

'For God's sake, Jemima, stop your dreaming and give me a sensible answer!'

The impatience in his voice brought her up short. He had got to his feet and was towering over her, so close that she couldn't look up at him without leaning backwards in her chair. She was aware of his elegance; he looked good in a dinner jacket. She had never thought much of grizzled hair before, but now she had to concede that it added a certain distinction to a man past his first youth. She wondered how old he was and because the wine had loosened her tongue from the discipline she imposed upon it, she opened her mouth to ask him, but catching his hard eye, said instead, quite meekly: 'Very well, Professor Cator, if Lady Manderly wishes me to go with her to Stratford-on-Avon, I will, on the understanding that I'm free to leave when she returns here, if I want to.'

'Good girl! I will take you home.' He frowned when he had said that because of the stricken look on her face—the girl hadn't got a home, had she?—but there was no need for him to feel sorry for her; he had cheerfully seen all the other companions go their solitary ways without a moment of regret.

'Thank you,' said Jemima with dignity, 'I can see myself back to my lodgings.'

He opened the door for her and followed her downstairs. The party was going well, the volume of noise deafened them as they reached the hall. Jemima said goodnight and went to the little cloakroom to fetch her coat, and when she came out he was waiting for her.

Belling, appearing in his silent way, opened the street door and the Professor followed her through and walked beside her in silence until she reached the shop entrance. Mrs Adams had given her a key for the night, and he took it from her, opened the door, switched on the light and stood aside for her to go past him. Just for a moment she thought that he was going to say something, but beyond a brief goodnight, he was silent.

CHAPTER FOUR

JEMIMA had meant to tell Mrs Adams of the Professor's suggestion at breakfast the next morning, but she was given no chance to do so. Her landlady and Shirley were far too busy asking her questions about the party. What was the food like, and the dresses, and what had Lady Manderly worn?

Jemima gave a detailed account of everything, beginning with the food and going on to Lady Manderly's purple satin and diamonds and as many of the dresses as she could remember.

'I didn't see very many guests,' she explained, which was true enough. She had wanted to see Gloria Egerton most particularly, but she hadn't had so much as a glimpse of her. She glanced at the clock. 'I must go, I'm going to be late and there's bound to be a lot of post to open.'

'O.K.,' said Shirley cheerfully. 'Perhaps the old lady'll let you off early on account of all that overtime you did.'

Jemima stacked her breakfast things neatly on the

draining board. 'Not likely!'

Lady Manderly was in a bad temper; she hadn't slept, she complained, her head ached, and then with the exception of one or two old friends she had found her guests tedious in the extreme.

'Never mind,' observed Jemima soothingly, opening envelopes and sorting the contents rapidly. 'You won't have to have another party until next year.'

'If I live as long,' declared her companion dramatically. 'I'm exhausted.' She put out a hand for the letters she was being offered. 'My nephew—Professor Cator, you know—has advised me to spend a few weeks quietly at a house I have in Warwickshire. I shall take his advice, since he seldom offers it, but when he does, it's to good purpose.' She went on surprisingly: 'I should like to give him some good advice too—to give up that silly little Gloria: feather-brained and wildly extravagant—he may be a wealthy man, but that's no reason for him to marry a careless spendthrift who thinks of nothing and no one but herself.'

Lady Manderly's massive bosom swelled alarmingly, but Jemima had her eyes lowered on to the letters in her hand, guessing that her employer was going to regret her words as soon as she had spoken them.

'I'm not quite myself this morning, Miss Mason, you will ignore what I have just said.'

Jemima said briskly: 'Certainly, Lady Manderly. Here's a letter from the caterers hoping you were completely satisfied with their services. What would you like me to say in reply?'

'Oh, say everything was as well done as possible, or something like that. Miss Mason, I wish to speak to you.'

Jemima raised quiet eyes to her employer's face. 'Yes, Lady Manderly?'

'I wish you to accompany me to Stratford-upon-Avon; you will of course live in the house, but I will continue to pay you your present salary on the under-standing that you will bear me company of an evening should I not have friends to dine or be going out myself. You will, of course, be free on Sundays as you are here, and you may continue to have a half day each week when it is convenient to me.' She added almost reluctantly: 'I hope you will come.'

'Thank you, Lady Manderly, I should like to. When do you plan to go?'

'At the end of the week. Do you drive a car?'

'Well, yes, of course.' Jemima added: 'But not at present—I—I haven't one now.'

'But you hold a licence? That's fortunate. As you know, I hire a chauffeur here, but at Roseleigh the gardener also drives the car. Usually he brings it here and drives me back, but that would be a waste of time and money; you shall drive the Daimler down.'

'Very well, Lady Manderly. Will Pooley be going with you?' Pooley was lady Manderly's maid.

'Naturally. When I go to stay in the country I do not rusticate, Miss Mason. You had better have your half day tomorrow, you will need to buy clothes. When there are no guests, I shall expect you to dine with me, and I dress for dinner.'

Jemima gave her a limpid look. 'I have a couple of quite suitable dresses, Lady Manderly, but I should be glad of an afternoon to make arrangements about my luggage. If we're to come back here in a month or so, I shall ask my landlady if she'll store my things.'

'Make any arrangements you think fit. In any case, I shall return here before Christmas.'

'Your house is in Stratford, Lady Manderly?'

'Yes, in the heart of the town, but in a quiet street

where few people go. I have a great many friends there, but life is very much quieter; a little bridge, small dinner parties—an evening at the theatre. You will probably have more time to yourself.'

Jemima picked up the newspaper. 'Yes, Lady Manderly.' Her voice was calm, her ordinary face composed, but inside she was excited. To be free to roam the streets of the town she knew so well, to go to Oxford once in a while, to go to the theatre perhaps . . . She had had a letter from Dick, full of praise of his new job, the people he had met, America with a big A; now she would be able to write back and reassure him that she too had found a pleasant niche in life. True, it would only last for a few weeks, but 'Sufficient unto the day' as her father would have said. She scanned the editorial, turned to the births and deaths columns, picked out the bits of news her employer might like to hear, and at that lady's command, began to read.

The day passed quickly enough, and since Lady Manderly declared that she was too tired to do more than go to bed early and have a tray in her room, Jemima found herself opening the shop door a good hour earlier than usual.

Shirley was behind the post office counter. 'Oh, good!' she exclaimed. 'Be a darling and hold the fort while I nip upstairs. I shan't be a minute and it'll only be papers and mags this time of day.'

She was a good deal longer than a minute. Jemima had sold almost all the evenings papers, several magazines and a couple of paper backs by the time she came back. 'Nice work,' commented Shirley cheerfully. ' 'Ow about putting in a bit of time in the shop when you're free?—we'd pay yer.'

It was an opening Jemima had hoped for and hadn't expected to get. 'That sounds a marvellous idea, only

I'll be away for a few weeks. I must tell Mrs Adams—Lady Manderly's going to Stratford-upon-Avon at the end of the week and wants me to go too . . .'

'Well, ain't that a bit of bad luck? Not counting on leaving us, are you?'

'I hope not. You know how happy I am here.' Which wasn't quite true, but after all Jemima had a feeling that she would never be quite happy again. 'I'd like to pay something for my room and leave my things here, if Mrs Adams wouldn't mind. If she wants to let the room, I could put everything in a cupboard.'

Shirley locked the door and put the 'Closed' sign up. 'Let's go and see what she says.'

Mrs Adams was quite prepared to look after Jemima's things while she was away, although she wouldn't promise not to let the room: 'Not that there's much call for lodgings this time of year and you won't be gorn all that time. Shall we say a pound a week to look after your bits and pieces?'

It seemed fair enough, and in any case there was no alternative. Jemima supposed she could have written to one of her friends in Oxford and asked them to keep her luggage, but pride prevented her from doing that. Everyone had been very kind when she and Dick had been left on their own, and for a little while helpful, but when they had moved to a flat, Jemima had guessed that their friends were relieved to see them go. Of course they wrote from time to time, but she had always been careful to answer their letters with a cheerfulness which, if not quite true, certainly left them with the impression that she and Dick were doing nicely.

The next morning passed peacefully enough. Lady Manderly seemed definitely subdued and even suggested that Jemima might leave for her half day directly after lunch instead of taking Coco for a walk first. And to Jemima's astonishment, as she was bidding her employer goodbye, Lady Manderly said quite mildly for her. 'I shall call you Jemima in future. You are still very young.'

Jemima spent the whole of her half day going through her wardrobe. She didn't possess many clothes, but those she had were well cut, of good material and well cared for; that they were also lacking in high fashion was obvious; they would look equally right in three years' time, even longer, and she was heartily sick of the whole lot. But new clothes were out of the question—she had had to buy shoes only last week and that had left her with a hole in her pocket. She washed and ironed and pressed and folded carefully, choosing a plain wool dress in a serviceable grey, a couple of skirts and a pair of slacks, blouses and sweaters and her two evening dresses, a rather prim brown jersey with a modest neckline and a sweeping skirt, and a patterned top and matching skirt—not the height of fashion but quite suitable for a companion. It was a pity that her winter coat was on its last legs, but it was elegant still and undateable, like everything else. How lovely, she thought, to buy something all the fashion rage and discard it the moment she was the least bit tired of it.

The days were getting shorter now, soon it would be cold. She added a couple of scarves and some warm gloves and thanked heaven that she had brought sensible shoes. Very soon now it would be November, and the old man who swept up the leaves from the road outside had told her only that morning that it was going to be an early winter with plenty of snow. It seemed a bit silly, as the sky was blue, even if a bit washed out, and only the early mornings were getting nippy, all the same she found her elderly leather boots and put them at the bottom of her case.

The next morning she was sent round to the mews behind the house and spent an hour with the Daimler. The hired chauffeur had been told to meet her there and greeted her with a cheerful scepticism. 'A bit big for a lady,' he pointed out. 'What've you been driving, miss?'

'A Volvo Estate, a Mini and sometimes a Land Rover.'

He looked at her with a tinge of respect. 'Lived in the country, miss?'

'Well, almost—Oxford actually, but I drove my father round a good deal. I haven't driven for some months, though, not since we've been in London, so I'd be glad of your advice.' She added: 'I'm not doing you out of a job, am I?'

'Lord luv yer, no, miss. I work for a Garage, y'see, go wherever I'm wanted. Lady Manderly always has me when she's in town, but there's plenty more like 'er.'

'Good. Now do tell me, which is the best way . . .'

They parted good friends with the promise that if Jemima liked to reach the garage by half past eight the next morning, he would let her drive the car. 'Just for 'alf an hour,' he told her. 'She runs like a dream, but you might like to get the feel of 'er.'

She managed very well, going through the early morning traffic with a calm which reassured the chauffeur. She stalled the engine just once as they were turning finally into the road where Lady Manderly lived. It was sheer bad luck that Professor Cator, scything his elegant way through the endless cars and taxis, should be directly behind her. She saw him in her mirror and waved him past her, ignoring his sour smile. Luckily she wouldn't see him before they left on the following day.

He was there early the next morning, walking in on them just as she was about to start on an account of some society wedding. She had just read the glowing description of what the bride wore when Lady Manderly interrupted her to say: 'Ah, Alexander—the Hockley wedding! The silly girl wore white—I don't know how she dared, with that frightful complexion of hers, and her first youth already far behind her.'

Her nephew bent to kiss her cheek. 'I was there—she looked quite nice, actually—hardly a beauty, but clothes help, of course.' His glance lingered for a moment on Jemima's Marks and Spencer blouse and skirt and she pinkened. His cool eyes watched the colour come and go. 'Good morning, Jemima, all ready to go, I hope?'

'Yes, thank you, Professor Cator.' She looked at Lady Manderly. 'Shall I come back presently, Lady Manderly?'

'No, certainly not. You can open the rest of these letters and get them sorted. Have you come to say goodbye, Alexander?' She added tartly: 'It's too early in the day for Gloria, of course.'

'Oh, yes. She doesn't surface until ten o'clock at the earliest. She sends her love. We might come down and see you—it's a pleasant run at this time of year. I must be off, I've a lecture to give very shortly.' He bent to kiss her again, nodded to Jemima and went off.

'I cannot think,' declared Lady Manderly, 'where Alexander gets his brains from. I know very little of what he does, but he's very much to the forefront in his work. All the same I can't think how he fills in his days.'

Jemima, curious by nature, had taken the trouble to

go to the public library and read up all about endocrinology. She had no doubt that the Professor was a
very busy man indeed, as well as being a clever one.
She had painstakingly worked her way through
detailed descriptions of all the glands involved, not
enjoying it all, and had come to the conclusion that
one gland would keep him busy enough and according
to her reckoning there were ten, all capable of getting
diseased, over-active, under-active or just not working.
She doubted very much if Lady Manderly would thank
her for telling her about them, and was surprised when
that lady exclaimed: 'Diabetes—I'm sure of that, because a friend of mine consulted him.'

'How interesting,' murmured Jemima. 'Is he a sur-
geon, Lady Manderly?'

'I believe not—he has rooms in Harley Street and I
suppose he goes to hospitals. He goes abroad sometimes—I daresay he finds his work interesting.'

Jemima murmured politely. She found his work
interesting too, and what was more, she was beginning
to find the Professor every bit as interesting as his
work. Not that she liked him in the least; aware of her
ordinary appearance, nevertheless she found it tiresome to be treated in an offhand manner. It would be
nice to get her own back, but she was too sensible a
girl to indulge in the impossible. She got on with her
morning's work, lunched off a tray because Lady
Manderly had guests for that meal, and presently at
the end of the day went back to the shop.

The drive down to Stratford-upon-Avon went off
without a hitch. Lady Manderly, installed in the back
of the car, dozed for a good deal of the journey, leaving
Jemima to drive unhindered out of London and on to
the M40, where she put her foot down and got up some
speed, expecting every moment to be told to slow

down, but surprisingly, Lady Manderly said nothing. Jemima skirted Oxford, feeling a pang of longing as she turned the car on to the A34 which would take them to Stratford-upon-Avon.

She knew the town well enough. She took the car over Clopton Bridge, turned left into Waterside and so to Southern Lane and then turned carefully into a narrow lane leading back towards the town centre. There were high brick walls here, and a glimpse of gardens and tiled roofs. She stopped halfway down before a pair of wooden gates, firmly shut. 'This is it, isn't it?' she asked Lady Manderly. 'I'll get someone to open up.'

There was a small door cut into the centre of one of the gates. She went through it and found herself on a cobbled sweep with out buildings on either side. A man came out of a half open door as she came to a halt and she said briskly: 'I've brought Lady Manderly—would you open the gates, please?'

The man nodded. 'That I will, miss. She wasn't expected so early, otherwise I'd 'ave had 'em open.'

He started to draw the bolts and Jemima took a quick look round. The drive was a short one, leading to a fair sized gabled house surrounded by velvety lawns and flower beds. The house was set at an angle to the road and she guessed that its door was just round the corner of the wall facing her; there would be a front path back to the road somewhere on the other side, although she couldn't see it either. Just as Lady Manderly had said, the house was secluded, and once inside the high walls they could have been in the heart of the country. And it was delightful to look at; typical of so many houses in that part of England with its whitewashed walls and oak beams and red-tiled roof. She went back to the car and drove through the gates, only half listening to the testy remarks made by her passenger about the delay, and up the drive to the front of the house and the front door, a solid oak one with a great iron latch and stout enough to withstand a siege. It was opened as she got out and a sharp-faced elderly woman came out on to the broad step.

'My lady—welcome, it's a pleasure to see you again.' She ignored Jemima and went past her to help Lady Manderly out of the car. 'You shall go straight to your room and I'll send up a tray—you'll be tired after your journey.'

'Ah, Spencer. No, I'm not in the least tired. We will lunch in the dining room in half an hour. See that our cases are taken up-stairs at once, will you? This is Miss Mason, my companion. My housekeeper, Mrs Spencer.'

She walked into the house, and Jemima and Mrs Spencer, exchanging guarded greetings, followed her. And although the housekeeper stood aside to let her enter the house, Jemima had the feeling that the woman regarded her with dislike. Natural enough, she thought, Mrs Spencer must have seen quite a number of companions go through the door.

The house was pleasant inside, furnished suitably with dark oak with polished floors and brocade curtains, and when she finally reached her own room she found it to be comfortable but quite impersonal, like a hotel bedroom. She wished she had brought a few of her own bits and pieces with her to make it seem more like home, then comforted herself with the thought that she would be at Stratford only for a month or six weeks. She unpacked her few things, tidied herself and went downstairs to wait for Lady Manderly. There was no one about and all the doors were shut. The first one she opened revealed the dining-room, rather gloomy by reason of the narrow latticed windows, made more so by the thick velvet curtains. She retreated and tried the door opposite—a sitting-room, gloomy too but much more cheerful by reason of the fire burning in the grate, its light gleaming on the polished furniture. There were easy chairs here, and a vast sofa and little tables bearing reading lamps. She advanced towards the fire, then gave a yelp as Professor Cator levered himself out of one of the chairs drawn up to it.

'You gave me a fright!' she squeaked accusingly. 'You could have said you were here . . .'

'I wasn't aware that I had to inform my aunt's companion of my whereabouts.' His voice was silky, and her gentle temper was stirred to wrath.

'What a perfectly beastly thing to say, and very rude besides. My old nanny would have washed out your mouth with soap and water . . .'

'So would mine! But I am no longer a small boy; I can say and do what I like. But I'll apologise if that will make you happy, Jemima. I can only say that you have the unfortunate effect of bringing out the very worst in me.' He looked at her with the faintest of smiles. 'You would do better to avoid me.'

She was retreating slowly backwards, intent on getting out of the room. 'Me avoid you!' I've never gone looking for you, you know, but I'll do my very best in future.'

'Do that. You drive very well for a woman, by the way.'

She had been on the point of a dignified exit, but she came to a halt. 'Why do you say that? You've never seen me drive.'

'My dear girl, I followed you for a good deal of the way this morning.'

She said indignantly: 'You didn't believe me when I

said I could drive the Daimler.'

'Oh, yes, I did—I always believe you, Jemima. Only most women have a different approach to driving a car. You, I am glad to see, drive like a man. I would even trust you with the Rolls.'

She let that pass. 'I didn't see you.'

He lifted his brows. 'Of course not, you don't suppose I travelled on your heels, do you? And for the last mile or so I took a different road.' He examined the nail of one hand. 'You really are a treasure, you know. We must keep you in the family.'

'No,' said Jemima. 'I daresay in your nasty arrogant way, Professor Cator, you mean that kindly. Nothing on earth would induce me to stay with Lady Manderly once we go back to London.'

'We are, of course, talking at cross purposes,' he observed blandly, 'but no matter. Why not sit down?'

She stood her ground. 'I'll let Lady Manderly know you're here.'

'Don't bother. She expects me to lunch.' He smiled at the relief on her face. 'No, you won't be having a little something on a tray in your room, Jemima, you're lunching with us.'

'Lady Manderly said that when she had guests she wouldn't expect me to have my meals with them.'

'Did she now? But I'm not a guest, am I? I'm afraid you'll have to bear with me, detestable though I am . . .'

Jemima opened her mouth to answer him back, quite heedless of the fact that she really had no business to talk to him as she was doing, but the door behind her was opened and Lady Manderly joined them.

'Ah, Alexander, how nice, dear. Lunch will be about ten minutes—just time for a drink. I'll have a sherry— a dry one.' She glanced at Jemima. 'You'd better have one too,' she said. 'I must admit that you drive quite well, Jemima.'

'Thank you, Lady Manderly.' Jemima accepted her glass without looking at the Professor and sat herself down in a composed manner at a little distance from the others, prepared to be civil but with no intention of joining in the conversation unless she was addressed. It was a pity, she mused, that there was no book on how companions should behave. She tended at times to forget that she was one—she had done just now, and heaven only knew what the Professor thought of her now. Not that it mattered one scrap what he thought, he was a thoroughly unpleasant man and she wished Gloria well of him. He'd be a ghastly husband—but then Gloria wouldn't make a very good wife. They deserved each other, thought Jemima, and looked up to find the Professor's eyes on her face, so that she went very pink indeed, imagining that he had known what she had been thinking.

They were served their lunch by a cheerful young girl who smiled in a friendly way at Jemima, and afterwards, when they had had coffee, Jemima was told that she might have an hour to herself. 'Come back here at three o'clock,' said Lady Manderly. 'Coco will need her walk.'

An hour wasn't long, but the house was within a few minutes' walk of the centre of the town, despite its seclusion. Jemima put on her jacket and let herself out of the house door. It was pleasant to have a little time to herself. She strolled down Sheep Street, looking in the shop windows, pretending to herself that she could buy anything she wanted. She walked as far as the post office and bought stamps; at least she would have something to write about to Dick. The clock was striking the hour as she went back into the sitting-room, and she was surprised at the pang of disappointment she felt when she saw that Lady Manderly was alone.

'There you are,' observed Lady Manderly in an admonishing tone, just as though she were late. 'Coco is quite ready for her walk. Take her along the river path, you can go past the Theatre and cross the bridge to the other bank.'

'Yes, I know, Lady Manderly,' said Jemima patiently. 'How long do you want me to walk her?'

'An hour will do. Be back here by four o'clock'.

How nice if Lady Manderly were to say please or thank you just once! It was surprising that she had so many friends, she was so ungracious. Jemima walked briskly down the lane to the Riverside, turned down by the theatre crossed the bridge and set off along the river. It was quite chilly now and the days were getting short. Christmas wasn't all that far away now; she wondered where she would be by then. Certainly not with Lady Manderly. Even if she had wanted to stay, the Professor's remarks had changed her mind for her. She would start looking for another job in good time before they returned to London. There was always the chance that one or other of their friends in Oxford would invite her for Christmas. They all knew by now that Dick was in America, and might think she would be on her own. In which case she could get a job directly after Christmas; she would have a little money saved by then, enough to pay for a bedsitter somewhere. The prospect was hardly exciting, so she didn't dwell on it but thought about Dick instead; he was happy and busy and content with his life in Boston. He had made friends too, so at least things were going well for him.

She turned round, the obedient Coco trotting beside her, and started back the way she had come. The river was delightful and now that it was getting towards dusk, the lights on the opposite bank looked inviting. Perhaps they would get a chance to go to the theatre, though she supposed Lady Manderly would go with her friends. All the same, she herself could go when she had a free afternoon—there were some matinees. She stopped to look at the theatre looming across the water; they were doing *The Winter's Tale* that week and *A Midsummer Night's Dream* the following week. She had seen the former and never liked the second, all those people milling round a wood, pretending not to see each other . . . *Richard the Second* would be nice, or *Othello*.

It was a loud whistling which disturbed her thoughts. The Professor's voice, over-hearty and loud, and still some yards away: 'You see how I am careful not to alarm you?' He had reached her as he was speaking, and she looked up at him in surprise. 'I thought you'd gone,' she said.

'Wishful thinking?' he queried blandly. 'I shall stay for dinner and drive back this evening. Tomorrow is Sunday, and I don't work then unless it's something urgent.'

'But don't you want to go back to . . .' Jemima paused and bit her lip. She had developed this bad habit of talking to this tiresome man as though she had known him for years.

'Yes?'

'Oh, nothing.' She saw the mockery in his eyes. 'Well, what I was going to say was, wouldn't you rather be with Gloria?' She added: 'It's none of my business.'

'No, it isn't. Isn't that beast ever allowed off her lead?'

'Lady Manderly said not . . .'

He took the lead from her and unhooked it, and

Coco, after one surprised look, flew off, racing like a mad thing along the footpath.

'Look what you've done!' exclaimed Jemima. 'She'll never come back!'

He let out a piercing whistle and Coco checked in her headlong run and came trotting back.

Jemima said coldly: 'Pure luck—she could have been the other side of the bridge by now.'

He flapped a large hand at Coco, who danced off again, and Jemima said with exasperation: 'There now, she's off again, and I've got to be back in a quarter of an hour.'

'Plenty of time—I'll walk with you, it's time we became acquainted. Tell me about your brother. I understand he is in the States?'

'Yes, he's in Boston—he's a scientist, not fully qualified yet, but he's done so well, he landed this job there. He can study further, of course, and get another degree in Natural Science. He's clever.'

He shot her a sidelong glance. 'And you?'

'Me? I'm not clever. Besides, when Mother was ill I took over the house.'

'So you are unqualified for a career of any sort? You won't, I presume, wish to stay as a companion for the rest of your life . . .'

She said snappishly: 'I could marry.'

'Ah, yes, you could.' His voice implied that he thought it highly unlikely. 'Of course, a job such as this one hardly allows you to save.'

'I manage—and I'm quite able to take care of myself, Professor Cator.'

'Er—no doubt. But you are quite unsuited to the post of companion, you know.'

Jemima felt a chilly hand on her spine. He was going to give her the sack; Lady Manderly was safely at

Stratford where she had any number of friends . . .

'You are wasted, Jemima. It is foolish of me to tell you this, for if you go I shall have the task of once more finding another woman to take your place. But it would be unfair to persuade you to stay—you could be earning three times as much if you trained for something worth while. All the same, now that I have said that, I hope that you will stay with my aunt until she returns to London.'

'I've already said I would.' Jemima, much astonished at this interest in her future, was staring at him, her mouth slightly open.

'Good.' He whistled again and waited while Coco came frolicking back to them. 'It's time we returned.'

He began to talk about the town as they walked back and then somehow she found herself telling him about her home in Oxford; she didn't realise just how much until they were crossing the bridge. She stopped in mid-sentence, her ordinary face pink and glowing with the pleasure of remembering. She said quite sharply: 'I'm talking too much, Professor. I'm so sorry, I quite forgot.'

'What did you forget, Jemima?' His voice was so soft that she answered without thinking.

'Why, that it's you I'm chattering to, and you're the last person . . .' She stopped again and went on guiltily: 'I'm sorry, I didn't mean to be rude, but we—we have nothing in common, have we? You're a learned Professor and I'm your aunt's companion and you don't like me.'

'Don't I?' His voice held surprise. 'Is that what you think?'

'Oh, it's quite all right, I'm not offended or anything like that,' she told him matter-of-factly. 'I saw that you didn't like me the very first time we met, only I just happened to suit, didn't I?'

'Indeed you do, Jemima. Do you think you'll be happy here? Mrs Spencer is rather a tartar, but it's all show and a sharp tongue.' They had reached the small gate leading up to the house from the lane and he opened it for her. 'We shall be dining a little earlier than usual, by the way; I've promised Gloria I'll take her to a party later on this evening.'

There was really nothing to say to that. Jemima murmured something and went ahead of him into the house where she took Coco along to the downstairs cloakroom to dry her paws. It was ridiculous that the thought of the Professor and Gloria going out on the town could depress her so much.

Once back in the house she was kept busy, not only attending to Lady Manderly's endless wants, but smoothing down Pooley's ruffled feelings. It seemed that she couldn't abide Mrs Spencer and since she had gone ahead of Jemima and Lady Manderly by train, she had had an hour or so in which to cross swords with that lady. Jemima, coming upon the two of them in a downstairs corridor, had contrived to settle their dispute at least for the time being, but she wondered, as she raced back upstairs with Lady Manderly's writing case, just how long the truce would last. She had been looking forward to her stay at Stratford; now she wasn't so sure. Besides, it was almost a hundred miles from London, and that was where Professor Cator would be. She pulled up short, horrified at her thoughts. Why on earth should she have allowed him to creep into her head? He would be well out of the way, and a good thing too.

Only first there was dinner to get through, with him sitting opposite her, casting what she imagined to be mocking glances at the brown jersey. But he took care

to include her in the conversation and as they got up
from the table she had to admit that he had delightful
manners when he chose to put himself out.

Dismissed for once quite pleasantly by Lady
Manderly, she bade them both goodnight and went to
her room. The Professor had got up and opened the
door for her, an old-fashioned courtesy she hadn't
expected, but he hadn't said anything. Not that there
was anything to say, she decided irritably as she undressed. She got into bed thinking about their walk by
the river. In retrospect it had been very pleasant, which
was surprising seeing that she disliked him so much.
She went to sleep frowning about it.

CHAPTER FIVE

JEMIMA found herself fully occupied during the next
few days. Lady Manderly, fired with a desire to see all
her friends again, made endless lists of people to be
invited to lunch or tea or to play bridge and then left
Jemima to telephone them, present her with the results
and then write more lists of the food she wished to be
served. But to her employer's demand that she should
see Mrs Spencer and tell her what she was to cook,
Jemima drew a firm polite line. 'It really wouldn't do,
Lady Manderly,' she told her pleasantly. 'Mrs Spencer
has been your housekeeper for a very long time, and
she expects to take her orders from you. If I ask her to
come and see you and write down all the suggestions
you've been making'—and they were legion—'I'm sure
you won't find it too tiring.'

Lady Manderly had given her a sharp look. 'Are

you and Spencer having trouble?' She wanted to know.

'Certainly not, Lady Manderly, but I have no wish to encroach upon her work.'

'H'm—you're the first companion I've had who didn't upset her to the point of giving notice.' She added grudgingly: 'Even Pooley likes you.'

'And I like Pooley—and Mrs Spencer. You're very fortunate to have such devoted people around you, Lady Manderly.'

Lady Manderly's face became suffused with dark colour. 'I am aware of their worth, and it's none of your business to remind me of it.'

Jemima had picked up the neat lists she had been making. 'Shall I fetch Mrs Spencer?' she asked. Her voice held the coaxing tones of someone humouring an ill-tempered child.

'Yes, you may do so.'

She was stopped at the door by Lady Manderly's voice, quiet for once: 'I hope . . .' She stopped and began again. 'You are really quite good at your job,' she allowed graciously.

And Jemima, going down to the kitchen to look for the housekeeper, found herself wishing she might stay with Lady Manderly indefinitely. But of course she wasn't going to, not after Professor Cator's remarks—besides, she had told him that she would leave when they went back to London and she had no patience with people who said one thing and did another.

Visitors started calling quickly enough. Jemima found herself having her lunch on a tray while Mrs Spencer, Pooley and the daily help coped with lunch for half a dozen ladies. On the second occasion of this happening she took her tray down to the kitchen and found that despite Mrs Spencer's stern rule, the place was in chaos.

'You need more help, don't you?' she asked the housekeeper. 'Tell me what I can do—Lady Manderly won't need me until her friends have gone.'

Mrs Spencer's eyes strayed to the dishwasher and before she could speak, Jemima said cheerfully: 'That's something I could manage . . .'

Mrs Spencer's severe face actually smiled. 'Well, it would be a great help. There's two extra for lunch we didn't know about.'

Jemima wondered who they were; there had been a Colonel and Mrs someone or other and a Mr and Mrs Plum—she remembered them because of the funny name, but since they were here they would have to be fed. She took an apron off the hook behind the kitchen door, swathed herself in it, and started to stack plates and bowls. The machine filled and doing its work, she turned to the glass and silver piled up by one of the sinks. Mrs Spencer was arranging coffee cups on a tray and Pooley was about to carry it upstairs while the daily help was taking off her overall and getting into her coat and jamming a forbidding hat on her head. She was a middle-aged body, hardworking, invariably silent and punctual, but nothing would induce her to stay one moment after her rightful working hours. She nodded briefly in the general direction of Mrs Spencer and Jemima and went out of the kitchen.

'Why don't you snatch something to eat?' asked Jemima, 'You must be famished. And another thing, Mrs Spencer, don't give me a tray again—why can't I come down here and have something with you? Then I'd be here to give a hand and you'd get a moment to yourself.'

'Well, I'm sure you're very kind, miss.' Mrs Spencer was pouring soup into a bowl. 'It's not always like this—it's just them two coming at the last minute. And I'm sure you've been ever so helpful with them lists— the other companions weren't no help at all, grumbled something awful if they didn't get their meals sent up on the dot and never set foot inside the kitchen.' She stirred her soup and looked thunderous. 'Not that I'd 'ave 'ad 'em here.' She saw the uncertain look on Jemima's face. 'Not meaning no offence, miss, you being so helpful. Of course you can 'ave something with us in the kitchen, though only when we're busy, mind you. Lady Manderly wouldn't like it.'

'She doesn't have to know, Mrs Spencer.'

They exchanged a speaking look before Jemima turned back to the sink.

She was gently washing Lady Manderly's silver when the kitchen door opened. Pooley with the coffee cups, which meant that she would have to hurry if she were to be available the moment her employer wanted her. She looked over one shoulder. 'Over here, if you don't mind . . .' and then stopped because it wasn't Pooley at all but the Professor. She turned her back on his stare at once and applied herself to the spoons, and he crossed to Mrs Spencer, who had got to her feet in a dignified flurry.

'Don't get up,' he begged her. 'I only came down to thank you for your trouble—we must have caused a good deal of bother.'

'Now as to that,' observed Mrs Spencer with a touch of her habitual tartness, 'you was unexpected, sir. Lucky I've got good 'elpers, and Miss Mason here giving an 'and.'

'You're short of staff?' he wanted to know. 'Surely you and Pooley don't do everything between you?'

'Well, no—Mrs Fox, she comes each morning, but she goes sharp on the hour, you see, and what with serving lunch and taking Miss Mason something on a tray . . . not that I grudge 'er that. I've just been telling 'er, she's a real 'elp to me.'

Jemima kept her back towards the pair of them. It was a pity that she had got to the end of the silver and there was nothing left to wash up. Now to get away with dignity and preferably invisible too . . . Pooley came unwittingly to her aid, coming through the door with a laden tray.

'There's my lady wanting you, miss.' Pooley sounded flustered. 'Getting a bit put out!'

Jemima whisked off the apron, dried her hands and pulled down her blouse sleeves with the speed of light. She was through the door and racing up the stairs before the Professor had time to do more than raise his eyebrows. She found Lady Manderly in the drawing-room, a little empurpled in the face, sitting very upright in an armchair, while Gloria lounged on one of the sofas. Jemima, coming to a quiet halt, nevertheless had time to inspect the quite perfect wool suit she was wearing; a delicate shade of blue, very impractical but definitely in the forefront of fashion, as was the blouse beneath it and the high-heeled Italian shoes. Jemima sighed inwardly and said in a calm voice: 'You wanted me, Lady Manderly?'

'Where have you been? My guests have been gone for ten minutes, you must have known I would want you for something or other. What have you been doing with yourself? Idling away my time and at my expense, no doubt!'

Jemima didn't answer. She wondered what had happened to upset Lady Manderly, because she was undoubtedly in a nasty temper. There was no point in making excuses and she had no intention of telling her that she had been doing the lunch dishes, although she had already resolved to hint, with great tact, that someone might be employed to take over from Mrs Fox, especially with all the extra work involved. Perhaps if Lady Manderly could be inveigled into the kitchen when everyone was at their busiest . . .

Lady Manderly was on the point of speaking when Gloria gave a shrill laugh. 'Poor Jemima, did you forget the time? Don't be hard on her, Lady Manderly—it must be deadly boring eating meals off a tray by oneself.' She opened her blue eyes very wide. 'Neither fish, flesh, fowl nor good red herring—that's you, isn't it, Jemima?'

Jemima turned her head and looked at Gloria, her face impassive, her eyes sparkling with rage, but nicely controlled. 'You are a very rude and ill-bred girl, Miss Egerton, but probably you don't know better.' She turned back to Lady Manderly, purple in the face again. 'When your guests have gone, Lady Manderly, perhaps you'll ring for me.'

She went without haste from the room, breathing rather hard, and bumped straight into Professor Cator, standing just outside the door.

'Do I detect temper beneath that calm, Jemima?' he wanted to know blandly. 'I admit that Gloria's description of your position here was hardly a tactful one, but she's very young and thoughtless.'

Jemima steadied her breath and spoke with only the faintest tremor. 'And you're middle-aged, and thoughtless and rude into the bargain, Professor Cator. I'm heartily sick of the lot of you!'

She flounced past him and up the stairs to her room where she had a short furious burst of tears, dried her eyes, made up her face and sat down to wait for Lady Manderly's summons.

It came some ten minutes later, and she went downstairs to the drawing-room, to find Lady Manderly still sitting in her chair, her colour now, thank heaven, as normal as it ever would be. She wasn't alone; Professor Cator was standing with his back to the window, his hands in his pockets, with no expression on his face at all.

'There you are, child,' declared Lady Manderly. 'My nephew wishes to speak to you before he goes.'

Jemima walked over to the window and stood in front of him. She could see the Rolls outside with Gloria sitting in the front seat, looking cross. She gave the Professor a coldly enquiring look and waited.

'I can't of course speak for Gloria,' he said gravely, 'but I do offer my sincere apologies for my rudeness and thoughtlessness, I cannot, alas, apologise for being middle-aged.'

His voice was as grave as his face, but she had the strong suspicion that he was laughing. She said, still very polite: 'Thank you, Professor Cator,' and closed her mouth firmly. She wasn't going to say that she was sorry for calling him rude and middle-aged; he was both, and he had admitted it, anyway. She glanced out of the window again and saw that Gloria was watching from the car. 'As for Miss Egerton, her opinion of me is of no consequence whatever.'

She stared at his tie, a nice rich silk one, and thought how priggish she sounded. He and Gloria would probably laugh themselves sick all the way back to London. He turned away without another word, kissed his aunt and went out of the room. She heard his voice in the hall and then the door shutting and a moment later the soft purr of the Rolls' engine. Wild horses wouldn't have made her look round.

She was startled to hear Lady Manderly chuckle. 'And that will give him something to think about!' she exclaimed with relish. 'My nephew is quite unused to opposition of any kind—and you called him middle-aged!' She chuckled again.

Jemima came from the window. 'Yes, I'm sorry about that, because of course he's not, but I was angry. I'll apologise next time I see him.'

'You'll do no such thing,' said her companion firmly. 'He is by no means a conceited man, but he is used to praise of his work and the attentions of I don't know how many vapid young women. He may even find it refreshing.'

Jemima thought this highly unlikely but she didn't say so. Instead she sat down to unpick some of Lady Manderly's tapestry work, which, as she frequently did, she had got all wrong.

It was getting colder. Jemima, walking Coco later that afternoon, shivered a little as she took the familiar path by the river. She should have tied a scarf round her head and worn her winter coat. She walked very fast so that Coco had a job to keep up with her, and when she saw the little dog's heaving flanks, apolo-gised. 'It's only because I'm a bit cold,' she explained, but there was another reason too; she was getting away from the day's events—indeed, more than that, she admitted to herself, getting away from all her memories of her encounters with Professor Cator.

'Horrible man!' she exclaimed loudly, and an old lady passing gave her a scared look and then glanced round just to make sure that there was no horrible man lurking among the bushes.

But the Professor, while not actually lurking in person, certainly had taken firm possession of her thoughts and wouldn't be shaken off. Jemima marched back into the house, handed over Coco to Pooley to be rubbed down and fed, and plunged into the numerous tasks waiting for her. She was sitting at a small table by the widow, sorting the household bills ready for Lady Manderly's perusal, when that lady observed, 'I shall be playing bridge tomorrow afternoon, so you may as well have your half day then, Jemima.' She put her lorgnette up to study the grocer's bill, which she considered excessive. 'You could call in and have this account checked while you're out and make an appointment at the hairdresser's for me . . .'

'I would like to go to Oxford,' said Jemima with placid firmness—a half day was a half day, after all, and they didn't come round all that often. 'By bus, you know.'

Lady Manderly peered at her and dropped her lorgnette, which Jemima picked up and handed back. 'A long journey, surely?'

'About an hour and a half. If I could leave directly after lunch, I should be there in plenty of time to spend the afternoon with some friends.'

Lady Manderly grunted and stretched out the hand for the coal bill. It was later that evening, as they sat at dinner, that she said suddenly: 'I've changed my mind about tomorrow, Jemima. I shall not play bridge, I shall go to Welford-on-Avon and visit some old friends. I shall want you to drive me there. We will go after lunch and remain for tea. They will be delighted to see me. It will of course mean that you can't have your half day, but you may have an entire free day next week—shall we say on Tuesday? That will give you a good deal more time to visit your friends in Oxford.'

Lady Manderly spoke in the self-satisfied voice of someone doing a great favour, and Jemima didn't argue. She was getting quite fond of her employer in a way; she was a domineering and selfish and demanding character, but perhaps she knew no better.

'That would be very nice, thank you. Welford is

about four miles' drive, isn't it?'

Lady Manderly looked surprised, and Jemima concluded that she had expected her to argue about the
change of plans. She helped herself from the dish of
caramel custard, one of Mrs Spencer's specialities,
which Pooley was offering her. After all, a whole day
in Oxford would be worth waiting for.

Welford was charming, with the river curling on
three sides of it and its long main street and village
green with the maypole. Lady Manderly's friends lived
in a pleasant old house at the end of the village, a size-
able Queen Anne gentleman's residence, with wrought
iron railings encircling the neat grounds and pristine
paintwork. Jemima, under orders from Lady
Manderly, got out and pulled on the iron bell pull by
the door and when it was opened up by a very old
man, told him who they were, feeling rather foolish
about it. But the old man's face lit up at once and he
hurried to the car to help Lady Manderly from it and
lead the way into the hall. Here he left them, saying
that he would tell the mistress at once, and Jemima,
taking advantage of the moment to themselves, asked:
'Shall I come back for you, Lady Manderly—if you'd
tell me what time . . .?'

'Certainly not. You will remain with me, Jemima.'
She had no time to say more, because a door had
opened and a very tall thin lady was bearing down upon
them. 'My dear Flo!' she exclaimed in a rather piercing
voice, 'what a delightful surprise—come in at once—
Blake, take Lady Manderly's coat.' She looked at
Jemima and Lady Manderly said: 'This is my companion, Jemima Mason. Mrs Walters, Jemima, a very
old friend of mine from schooldays.'

Jemima said how do you do in her pleasant voice
and followed the two ladies into a large drawing-room,

occupied by an old gentleman, two cats sitting side by side before a blazing fire, and a Jack Russell terrier sitting at the old man's knee.

The old man didn't get up and she saw that there were two sticks propped against his chair, but he held out both hands to Lady Manderly, who took them in hers, exclaiming: 'John, you haven't changed at all—it must be quite a year since we saw each other last.'

'And you're more handsome than ever,' he assured her. 'And who's the nice little thing with you?'

'My companion, Jemima Mason . . .'

'Not a bit like the last one,' declared the old gentleman, and put on his glasses in order to examine Jemima better. 'Looks a lady too.'

Jemima found Mrs Walters beside her. 'Don't be vexed, my dear—my husband has always said exactly what he thinks, and it's sometimes a little embarrassing.' She took her arm. 'Come and meet him—he likes a new face.'

Driving back later, Jemima had to admit that she had enjoyed her afternoon. For one thing, it was nice to be accepted without any snide remarks, and it was nice to have it taken for granted that she would have tea with everyone else and not on the inevitable tray in another room. She only wished that Lady Manderly would be struck by the same idea.

That was too much to expect. For the next two days she lunched in the library off trays brought to her by the new daily help who had miraculously joined the household two days earlier, while Lady Manderly entertained her friends in the dining-room. It was a relief that the next day was Sunday and she would be away almost all day visiting a distant relation in the town. All Jemima would have to do was drive her there, and collect her again when she was told to. She was, of course, given several jobs to do while her employer was away and there was Coco to take for a walk, but she went down to the kitchen to have her lunch, and being the kind of person to get on with everyone, she enjoyed every minute of it. When she had gone back upstairs, Mrs Spencer and Pooley, for once seeing eye to eye, agreed that she was ever such a nice young lady; no airs and graces either. 'Not like some I could mention,' said Mrs Spencer darkly. 'I wouldn't work for 'er—not for all the tea in China I wouldn't. I'm right sorry for the Professor—if 'e's not careful, 'e's going to make a fine old rod for his own back.'

The two ladies, the hatchet buried for the moment, settled down to a pleasant gossip.

Jemima, her chores done, settled down to write letters—a long one to Dick, and a shorter one to Shirley and Mrs Adams. And that done, she put on her coat and took Coco for another walk, only a short one this time, though, because Lady Manderly might ring for her to go along and collect her. Round about teatime, she had said; Jemima hoped devoutly that she would be able to have her tea first. A hope fulfilled, with half an hour to spare.

On Tuesday it poured with rain, but Jemima had no intention of that spoiling her day. She put her week's pay into her shoulder bag, got into the sensible shoes, and suitably although not fashionably dressed, tapped on Lady Manderly's bedroom door. Pooley answered, opening the door a crack as though there was a tremendous secret she was guarding with her life.

'Morning,' said Jemima cheerfully. 'Please will you tell Lady Manderly that I've just gone and I'll be back about nine o'clock this evening.'

Pooley nodded. 'Yes, miss,' and then in a whisper:

'There'll be some soup in the kitchen if you're hungry.'

Jemima grinned her thanks. 'I won't wait,' she said softly, 'I want to get the bus.'

She sped away, bent on getting out of the house before Lady Manderly had one of her changes of mind and demanded her attendance.

The bus was only half full. She had a seat to herself and sat watching the familiar countryside, and once in Oxford itself, she wasted no time but started to walk along familiar streets, pausing at each well-remembered spot; the Radcliffe Camera, Christ Church Tower, Balliol, Brasenose, Oriel—she visited them and many more until she realised suddenly that she was quite famished. She knew most of the cafés and restaurants in the city, and she went to a small Italian restaurant in Magdalen Street, to find to her delight that the proprietor remembered her and her brother. He served her himself with a risotto made to his own secret recipe, following it with a spectacular ice cream and a pot of coffee which he shared with her. It was like old times, and just for a little while she was completely happy. Only when she was out in the street again some of the happiness ebbed away, but she caught the tail end of it, told herself not to wallow in self-pity and walked down through the streets until she reached her old home. Perhaps it was silly of her to want to see it again, to awaken pleasant memories—she wasn't sure. She turned away after a few minutes and started the short walk to the house of old friends. She hadn't really intended to visit them, but it would be nice to catch up on events, even though she and Dick had been away for some time now. She glanced at her watch as she knocked on the door; she had a couple of hours before the bus went; she hoped they'd ask her to stay to tea.

They did, delighted to see her, although she saw quickly enough that they didn't really want to know if she and Dick were managing or not. She touched very lightly upon her job because although they had asked her what she was doing, they expected a reply which wouldn't disturb their pleasant calm life. Dick was another matter, of course. She could enlarge upon his success and his job in Boston, and they sat back, Mr and Mrs Gibbons, their married daughter Joan and Philip, their only son, looking smugly pleased, as though it was by their efforts he was there. Jemima didn't blame them, their peaceful little world was so far removed from her own. It was when the door was flung open and a young man breezed in that the peace was shattered—nicely so, but shattered nonetheless.

'My nephew, Andrew Blake,' said Mr Gibbons. 'He's staying with us for a few weeks—over from New Zealand.' And as the young man crossed the room: 'This is Jemima Mason, the daughter of an old friend of ours, come to see us. And I hope she'll come frequently while she's so close to Oxford.'

Jemima smiled and shook hands. He was the first young man she had had a chance to speak to for ages and he looked nice—open, rugged face, blue eyes, fair hair, not tall but well built. For no reason at all she had a vivid picture of another face, topped by grizzled hair, the mouth mocking her, the eyes cold. She dismissed it firmly, accepted another cup of tea and allowed herself to be chatted up by Andrew. It made a nice change from cold snubs.

She got up to go presently; she had plenty of time for her bus, but there was such a thing as outstaying one's welcome, and she did want to come again. Andrew got up with her. 'My car's outside,' he declared, 'I'll run you back,' and despite her protests he joined in her goodbyes and went outside with her. The car was an old Triumph, an open model with the hood down. Jemima prudently tied her scarf round her head and got in. It would be a chilly ride, no doubt, but a nice change from the bus.

Andrew liked to drive fast. Once free of Oxford he zoomed along, talking non-stop, quite often with his head turned towards her, so that, although she wasn't a nervous girl, she itched to put a hand on the steering wheel. He talked about everything under the sun and in such a friendly way that she found herself warming to him, and when he suggested that they might go to the theatre one evening, she agreed without hesitation. 'Though I never know from one day to the next when I'll be free,' she explained.

'Give me a ring, then,' he suggested. 'Let's make it next week, whenever you get your half day. With luck I'll be able to get two seats at short notice. I'm not a real enthusiast about Shakespeare, but I don't dare to go back home without having been to see at least one of his plays. Do you know what's on?'

Jemima frowned in thought. 'Next week? Well, there's *Much Ado About Nothing* and *Hamlet*. I hope it'll be *Hamlet* . . .'

'Make's no odds to me,' said Andrew, and put on a burst of speed to overtake a transport ahead of him. That there was a car coming towards them flashing lights indignantly didn't seem to bother him at all.

Jemima let out a held breath. 'Yes, well—I'm sure you'll enjoy it. The Royal Shakespeare Theatre is famous, so are the people who act there.'

'I'll collect you in time for a meal first—any ideas about where to eat?'

'There's a good restaurant at the theatre, you can either eat before the play starts or when it's finished.

That's a bit late, though.'

'Your old dragon keeps tabs on you? We'll eat first, then. I'll give you Uncle's phone number.'

'I know it; I've known them almost all my life, they were close friends of my mother and father, you see.'

'Mother and father dead?' He sounded casually kind. 'Sorry about that. All on your own, are you, with your brother in the States?'

'Well, not really, I've got a job and digs in London.'

'Sounds drear. We must make up for that while you're in Stratford. How long do you think you'll be here?'

'A month—six weeks. I really don't know.'

He had slowed, to her relief, as they crossed the bridge over the Avon and started up Bridge Street. 'Plenty of time to get acquainted,' he told her on a laugh, and Jemima agreed, laughing too. It was good for her ego to have a young man even faintly interested in her—after all, during the last few weeks Professor Cator had flattened it almost beyond repair.

They were going slowly through High Street and Andrew pulled up in front of a still open café. 'How about a cup of coffee?' He glanced at his watch. 'It's only just after seven o'clock.'

It seemed a long time since her lunch and Mrs Gibbons' tea had been very dainty; perhaps he would suggest a sandwich to go with it ... He didn't, not even a biscuit; probably it wouldn't enter his head that she might be hungry. They didn't hurry, but when they got up to go he looked at his watch again. 'Well, all good things come to an end,' he told her, and gave her a charming smile. 'Aunt has supper at nine o'clock, I'll miss it if I don't drop you off and race for home— she's a fabulous cook, and I happen to know it's steak and kidney pie!'

Jemima's mouth watered. She supposed he thought everyone had supper at nine o'clock. Well, she could always creep down to the kitchen and get that soup. She got into the car and directed him down Chapel Street and into Chapel Lane. The gates were open and although she asked him to put her down outside them he laughed and turned the car through them, roaring up the drive much too fast and far too loudly.

'Might as well have a look at the place now I'm here,' he told her easily, and skidded to a halt in front of the door.

The door was shut, thank heaven, but the heavy curtains hadn't been drawn over the downstairs windows, and both the dining-room and the drawing-room were brightly lit. Lady Manderly hadn't said anything about guests for dinner.

'Any chance of coming in and having a look round?' asked Andrew.

Jemima glanced at him, appalled. 'Heavens, no—I mean, it's a private house.'

'We're more hospitable in New Zealand.' He got out and she got out too.

'Thank you for the ride,' she said a little shyly, 'and the coffee. I enjoyed it.'

He eyed her smilingly. 'Don't get much fun, do you?' He tucked a hand under her arm. 'We'll change all that.' He turned her round to face him and kissed her roughly, and she turned her face away just in time to offer him a cheek.

Andrew laughed. 'A bit out of practice?' he asked cheerfully; his hearty voice sounded very loud in the quiet garden. Jemima hoped most fervently that no one could hear—or see, for that matter. All those windows . . .

Her hopes were in vain. She hadn't noticed that the

door had been opened and that someone was standing in its shadow, watching. Still unaware, she wished Andrew a sober goodnight, watched while he roared away from the house and turned to go indoors.

It was only then that she saw Professor Cator standing there. He didn't say anything at first, but his smile was nasty, so she judged it expedient to pass him with the smallest nod, and go up smartly to her room. She was stopped; he was a large man, one step sideways and her way was blocked.

'I'm surprised,' observed the Professor silkily. 'You don't look that kind of a girl.'

Jemima, forced to stay where she was, asked warily: 'And what do you mean, Professor?'

'The kind of girl to have such a—shall we say, boisterous?—boy-friend.'

'He is not my boy-friend. I met him for the first time this afternoon.' She could have bitten out her tongue, because he pounced on that at once.

'Surely not a pick-up?' he asked smoothly. 'Perhaps this rigorous life style you lead here has driven you to extremes?'

'I should like to slap your face!' said Jemima, glowing with splendid rage, then found herself on the verge of tears when he leaned down and offered one side of a massive jaw. She said in a little voice: 'I don't know why you needle me, Professor Cator. Isn't it enough not to like me and let me keep out of your way?'

He straightened up. He said in a surprised voice: 'I do believe that it's too late for that, Jemima,' and stood aside to let her pass into the hall. She was almost at the stairs when he asked: 'Have you had anything to eat?'

She told herself that she was no longer hungry even while her insides rumbled a denial. She would rather starve than be beholden to him, even for a crust of bread. She was aware that she sounded a little dramatic even in her thoughts, but it suited her mood. She said quietly: 'I don't need supper, thank you,' and went on up the stairs.

Still furiously angry though she was, her thoughts kept dwelling on hot soup, a great plate of chips, rolls and butter, lavish cups of coffee . . . They almost but not quite eclipsed the Professor.

She had a bath and got into bed and tried to take comfort from the luxury of her surroundings—after all, she was warm and the bed was soft and cosy and she still had a good bit of her book to read. She punched up her pillows and settled herself against them and opened it, but a couple of pages sufficed to show her that the heroine was a fool and the hero too soppy for words. She flung it down, and at the same time someone knocked on the door.

It was barely nine o'clock, surely Lady Manderly didn't expect her to present herself at that hour? Come to think of it, she hadn't seen any cars. If there weren't any guests, she was supposed to play cards or something similar with her employer—did that apply to her half day?

She called, 'Come in,' in a questioning voice and Pooley came round the door with a tray.

'The Professor,' she explained. 'He said he'd been in the hall when you came back and he didn't think you looked quite the thing, asked if we'd bring you up a little something . . .' She smiled quite kindly and put the tray on the bedside table. 'Said he thought you might have gone up to bed so as not to bother anyone. Well, me and Mrs Spencer knows that's more than likely, you being so considerate and all. It's just a snack so that you'll sleep well. Did you have a nice afternoon?'

'Yes, thank you, Pooley.' Jemima had an awful feeling that she was going to burst into tears, but she managed to smile instead. 'You're both so kind, and I'll eat every scrap.'

'That's right, miss. The morning 'll do for the tray.'

There was soup and a cheese soufflé, so light it almost flew from the dish, and a peach to follow as well as a pot of coffee. Jemima cleared the lot and felt marvellous afterwards, only for some reason she cried herself to sleep.

CHAPTER SIX

LADY Manderly made no reference to Jemima's day. The moment Jemima put her head round the sitting-room door, she embarked on her usual morning activities without one single enquiry as to whether she had enjoyed her freedom. Not that Jemima had really expected it; Lady Manderly was concerned only with herself and her own comfort and wellbeing, although she doubted if she would really be deliberately unkind; it was just that she had never considered anyone else but herself, and it seemed a little late in life to change now. She didn't mention her nephew's visit either, but there again, she would consider it was none of Jemima's business, as indeed it wasn't.

The rest of the week passed peacefully enough, not that living with Lady Manderly was entirely peaceful; Jemima was glad to retire to her room each evening, for except on the occasion when her employer went out to dinner with friends, she bore that lady company,

first at a long-drawn-out dinner and afterwards in the
drawing-room, playing bezique or, what was more
exhausting, listening to Lady Manderly's long-winded
opinions about one thing and another. She was a lady
of decided views and objected strongly to anyone op-
posing them, so that the unfortunate listener was held
captive and unable to say a word in dissent. Jemima,
inclined to be argumentative by nature, found it all
very trying.

But there were compensations; she enjoyed her walks
with Coco, and often enough she was sent into the
town to post letters, match embroidery silks or pur-
chase books, which gave her an opportunity to look in
the shop windows and decide what she would buy
when she had enough money.

The temptation to get herself another dress for the
evening was great. The brown was definitely dowdy
and the separates, while passable, were being worn far
too often. But she had made up her mind to save
enough money to live on while she found another job
in London, and she wasn't sure how long that might
take. She had been lucky getting this one, next time
might not be so easy. She promised herself that she
would save her first three weeks' money and then do
some spending.

It wasn't until the weekend that Lady Manderly
mentioned casually that Jemima might have her half
day on the following Wednesday, and Jemima lost no
time in phoning the Gibbons' house. Andrew wasn't
there, so she left a message and then waited a whole
day before he phoned back. It was a pity that she was
in the middle of reading the day's news out loud when
the phone rang. Conscious of Lady Manderly's beady
eyes upon her, she said 'Yes,' and 'No' and 'Thank
you very much,' terrified that the old lady would hear

Andrew's hearty voice bellowing that he supposed she was being prim because the dragon was eavesdropping.

'Half past seven,' she said in answer to his enquiry as to when the play started, and then, 'Very well, half past six in the foyer.'

'And who was that?' enquired Lady Manderly, awfully.

'A friend who's at Oxford. He's invited me to the theatre on Wednesday evening.' Jemima picked up *The Times* again and continued reading about the fuel crisis. She read very nicely, her quiet voice giving no sign of her excited thoughts. An evening in Andrew's company would be delightful, she repeated the thought a shade too emphatically.

It would have to be the wool dress, she decided as she got ready on Wednesday evening. She had worn the suit when she had gone to Oxford and a long skirt would be a bit much, especially as she didn't know where they were to sit. Dressed, she examined herself in the pier glass in her room and then turned away with an impatient sigh. She looked neat, that was the best she could say for herself. She only hoped that Andrew wasn't a connoisseur of women's clothes.

He was waiting for her in the theatre foyer, and one glance at his face warned her that he was agreeing wholeheartedly with her own opinion of her appearance. She greeted him serenely, wondering miserably if he would ever ask her out again, while she cast covert glances at the well dressed women around them. It depended on how much he liked her, she supposed, and thus challenged, worked hard at being the perfect companion; a good listener, ready to laugh when called upon, keeping up her end of the conversation. It was

exhausting as well as tiresome; she had wanted to see
Hamlet very badly, but it wasn't Andrew's idea of an
evening out—that was obvious after the first ten
minutes; he muttered asides, coughed and looked
around him, and his sigh of relief when the curtain
came down for the interval and they went with
almost everyone else to the bar was exaggeratedly
loud.

Jemima did her best, but he didn't want to discuss
the play or the actors, so she led the conversation round
to New Zealand while she sipped her sherry and he
described his town, Kiakoura. She wasn't at all sure
exactly where it was, and she didn't like to ask. She
murmured politely when he paused for breath, but he
didn't really need her to talk, just as long as she
listened. It was bliss to go back to Shakespeare's world,
but she felt guilty for the rest of the evening. Andrew
had asked her out and she felt that she was giving him
a poor return for his money; she didn't even look attractive, and she found, over their supper after the
play, that it was increasingly difficult to find a topic
which they could talk about with real interest. It
dismayed her to discover that they really had nothing
in common.

Supper was delicious and Andrew was impressed by
the restaurant, half way up the great curving stone
staircase. It was almost full, too, and the atmosphere
was pleasant. Jemima would have liked to have discus-
sed the play, but Andrew had dismissed her first
tentative remarks with a vigorous: 'Well, so that's
Shakespeare, is it? Myself, I'd rather have a good mus-
ical show. I'm going up to town next weekend—a pity
you can't come, we might have taken in a couple of
theatres.'

But he hadn't asked her, thought Jemima, and

realised that he hadn't intended to. She hadn't come up to expectations, she knew that, and she did her best to make up for it by listening to another long description of the country round his home and the sheep-farming there. The unbidden thought that Professor Cator would have been a far more agreeable companion quite shook her, and made her even more attentive.

They walked back presently and this time he didn't come up to the house, but wished her a cheerful, careless goodbye at the gate with no mention of a further meeting. She hadn't expected that anyway.

The house was quiet as she let herself in with the key she had been allowed to borrow. She turned off the lamp in the hall and went softly upstairs. Lady Manderly's bedroom door was ajar with light streaming on to the landing. Jemima was almost past it, walking on tiptoe, when she heard the old lady's voice which bade her enter.

'Come in, Jemima. There's no need to creep about the house in that fashion.'

Jemima did as she was bid. She might have pointed out that she was being considerate in a sleeping household, but she held her tongue. Getting the better of the old lady was very nearly impossible. She closed the door behind her and waited.

Lady Manderly looked just as formidable in her bed as she did out of it. Her taste ran to satin and lace and plenty of both—she was festooned in them, so was the bed. Jemima, whose heart was soft, found it rather pathetic, although there was nothing in the old lady's manner to warrant sympathy.

'Well,' said Lady Manderly, peering at Jemima through her lorgnette, 'did you enjoy your evening?'

'Yes, thank you. The play was quite splendid, and I liked the way they did it—with no real scenery . . .'

She was interrupted. 'And the young man? Did he enjoy it?'

'Well, up to a point. I think he prefers something a bit more lively.'

Her companion snorted. 'And when is he taking you out again?'

'He isn't. He's going to London for a visit.'

'But he'll return?' went on Lady Manderly, remorselessly questioning.

'Well, yes, I expect so.'

'But you don't expect to see him again?'

Jemima shook her head and the old lady nodded hers in a satisfied fashion. 'I'm not in the least surprised. He's not for a girl such as you.' She threw a penetrating glance at Jemima. 'You're not upset, I hope?'

'Not in the least, Lady Manderly,' said Jemima placidly, and meant it.

'I'm counting upon you not getting involved with a man during the next few weeks,' observed Lady Manderly. The way she said it, it sounded like an order.

'I'm not very likely to do that.' Jemima felt as though she were stating the obvious. 'Can I get you anything before I go to bed?'

'Nothing, thank you. Tomorrow I wish you to drive me into the town. I have several purchases to make. Goodnight, Jemima.'

Dismissed with a wave of the lorgnette, Jemima said goodnight and went out of the room, shutting the door quietly behind her. In her own room she undressed slowly, sat for a long time before her dressing table mirror studying her reflection, and then got into bed. The evening had hardly been a sparkling success: Andrew had found her dull, she suspected, and she was quite prepared to admit that probably she was.

Certainly she hadn't been at ease with him; hearty types were fine taken in small doses, but she preferred someone a little quieter. And with that thought a very clear picture of Professor Cator presented itself behind her closed lids.

'Go away,' said Jemima crossly. 'I don't like you in the least!'

She thumped her pillows and buried her head in them to shut him out. By concentrating on Dick's success in Boston and planning a visit there, she managed to ignore him, and presently went to sleep.

Lady Manderly made no further reference to Jemima's visit to the theatre. The morning was spent driving her from one shop to the next, helping her out of the car and then in again, and on several occasions being commanded to accompany her into whichever shop she happened to be visiting. The last shop they visited was a boutique, a very superior one, all grey velvet, long mirrors and svelte sales ladies. Lady Manderly spent a long time there, looking at evening stoles, gossamer things made of sequined tulle and lace, guaranteed to make any female feel attractive, even if she wasn't. Lady Manderly bought two finally and Jemima, making out the cheque for her to sign, thought of all the clothes she could have bought with the cost of them. It was a lovely shop, spilling over with the kind of clothes she would love to wear. She didn't allow the thought to sour her but took possession of the elegant package, settled Lady Manderly in the car, and got in herself. She hoped they would go back to the house now; she was hungry and a little tired; her employer was no light weight when it came to getting her out and into the car a dozen times or more. Besides, they hadn't had coffee. She sat behind the wheel and waited to be told where to go next.

'Home, Jemima—I have a guest for lunch.'

Something on a tray, reflected Jemima. Perhaps I could slip down to the kitchen, though . . .

'You will lunch with us.'

'Very well, Lady Manderly.' It would be another of her old friends, supposed Jemima. They would talk about their childhood and their families and now and again, when they remembered, they would say something to her. It was only a little less lonely than having lunch off a tray with a book propped up in front of her.

She was to be in the sitting-room at a quarter to one; she did her face and her hair, took a quick look at her appearance, adequate enough in a good tweed skirt and a silk shirt blouse, and took herself downstairs. There was a busy afternoon ahead of her—letters to answer, several phone calls to make, cheques to make out for Lady Manderly to sign, Coco to take out for a walk, and as there were no guests for dinner that evening, she would be playing cribbage or bezique after dinner. Perhaps she would have time to write some letters while Lady Manderly rested before dinner. Dick of course, and the Gibbons, with some excuse as to why she wouldn't be going to Oxford again, and Shirley . . . Shirley wrote each week, full of questions all of which had to be answered. At least this week there was the theatre to write about.

Jemima went into the sitting-room exactly on time and found Professor Cator standing in front of the fire. His long thoughtful look wasn't particularly friendly, nor was his, 'Good afternoon, Jemima,' and she stood looking back at him wordlessly so that after a moment or two he asked coldly: 'Why do you stare so?'

She couldn't answer that. Perhaps Gloria or one of her type would have known what to say, but she didn't.

She wondered how he would react if she told him that she had just discovered that she had fallen in love with him; that she didn't dislike him in the least; that his arrogance, his mocking manner, his cold civility—even harder to bear—were quite swallowed up by her love. She imagined his reply to that and went bright pink, which made matters much worse, for he lifted his eyebrows in a hateful manner and smiled faintly.

She hoped the thudding of her heart couldn't be heard in the quiet room. 'You surprised me.'

The eyebrows went up again. 'Indeed? And yet I'm no stranger to my aunt's house.' He added silkily: 'And shouldn't the perfect companion be beyond surprise?'

A splendid rage fought with her love. 'You're being rude again,' she told him severely.

'Naturally—you expect it of me.' He turned to greet his aunt as she came into the room and Lady Manderly offered a cheek for his kiss.

'I'm glad you could come, Alexander. I need your advice about some shares.' She accepted a sherry and when he had handed a glass to Jemima he said:

'Well, I can't stay long, Aunt. I've a lot of work on hand for the next few days. I must leave in a couple of hours.'

'Then we'll have a little chat directly after lunch. Jemima, go and fetch the papers on my desk in my bedroom and put them here on a table.'

Jemima put down her drink and went away. She was quite glad to go, for it gave her a minute or two to pull herself together. She felt bemused and quite bewildered and, contrary to what she had expected, not in the least happy. To get away from the Professor as soon as possible was the obvious answer, and when she got back to the sitting-room she suggested in her calm way that since Lady Manderly wanted to discuss private matters with her nephew, would it not be a good idea if they were to lunch alone?

Aunt and nephew both looked at her. 'Certainly not! I never discuss money matters at table—besides, I'm sure Alexander would like to hear your opinion of the play you went to.'

A look at his face convinced her that it was the last thing he wanted to talk about. Wild horses, let alone Lady Manderly, wouldn't make her tell him anything. She sat sedately at the small table in the dining-room and beyond answering when spoken to, had nothing to say for herself.

Directly the meal was over, she excused herself on the plea of phone calls to make on behalf of her employer, who reminded her that when that had been done, she should take Coco for her walk. 'And be back by half past three, Jemima,' ordered Lady Manderly. 'There are several household bills for you to deal with.'

Jemima didn't look at the Professor when he got up and opened the door for her; she said, 'Thank you,' in his general direction and jumped smartly across the hall to the sitting-room, where she closed the door, dealt with the phone calls in a businesslike manner, and then opened the door again and peered round it, not wishing to meet Professor Cator again. There was no one about, so she went to her room, put on her coat and went in search of Coco. The little dog was in the kitchen, lying by the Aga, but she came prancing across to Jemima and allowed her lead to be fastened and since the household staff were all in their sitting-room, having a short rest before tackling the post-lunch chores, Jemima slipped out of the kitchen door, round the side of the house, and down the path into the lane— watched, if she did but know it, by the Professor, standing at the drawing-room window, listening with half an ear to his aunt's diatribe against stockbrokers.

It was a blustery autumn day and Jemima walked quickly along the well known path. The river looked cold and sluggish and there weren't many people about, although on the other side of the water she could see people going in and out of the shops in High Street and Sheep Street. She didn't look after a while; it made her feel lonely, and she was quite glad when it was time to return to the house.

She got to the door with a few minutes in hand. Lady Manderly might have said be back by half past three, but Jemima knew from previous occasions that what she really meant was be back in the sitting-room, Coco disposed of, and ready to work, at that hour. She put a hand on the door handle, but someone from the other side opened the door first—the Professor, ready to leave. She had expected that he would be gone. There was no sign of his car, but perhaps he had left it at the end of the drive and she hadn't thought of looking there.

He stood back to let her pass and then put out a hand to catch her by the arm so that she was forced to stand still. He said without preamble: 'Gloria and I will be coming for the weekend,' and then: 'How very alive you look, Jemima.' He bent and kissed her on her astonished mouth and went past her without a backward glance. She stood watching his vast back disappearing down the drive, and only when he was out of sight did she shut the door. 'What an extraordinary man,' she confided to Coco, and then as the grandfather clock in the hall struck the half hour, ran down to the kitchen with Coco under one arm.

'I'm late,' said Jemima to Mrs Spencer. 'Be a darling and wipe her paws.' And she fled back up the stairs to her room, flung off her coat, ran a comb through her hair and presented herself, a little out of breath still and not altogether because she was hurried, at the sitting-room door.

'Late,' declared Lady Manderly, and sounded pleased that she could find fault. 'Why?'

'I don't really know, Lady Manderly, and I can't think of an excuse.'

Lady Manderly blinked. 'Are you being impertinent?'

'Certainly not, Lady Manderly. What would you like me to do first?'

Her employer snorted. 'These accounts. Get them added up, will you, and fill in the cheques. I have two friends coming to tea, so you may have yours here, Jemima.'

A state of affairs which suited Jemima very well. She wanted time to think about the Professor, and just why he had kissed her. All in the same breath, as it were, as the mention of Gloria. Left to get on with her reckoning, Jemima started to plot as to the chances of getting a half day on Saturday—she would be free on Sunday anyway and then she wouldn't need to see either Gloria or Professor Cator. It would mean having her meals out, but that couldn't be helped.

The new daily help came in with her tea presently, Coco at her heels, and Jemima took the tray to the fire and shared Mrs Spencer's delicious scones with the little dog, and because Lady Manderly liked to talk politics, carefully conned *Today in Parliament*. It was as well that she did, for dinner was entirely taken up with her employer's forceful opinion about politicians. She didn't need much in the way of replies, but it helped if one could keep track of what she was talking about. Jemima was rewarded by a: 'You are an intelligent girl, Jemima, and you seem to have a grasp of present-day politics.' Lady Manderly rose from the table. 'Do you play the piano? I have neglected to ask you this, but so few modern young women do.'

'Well, I do—not very well, though.'

'I should enjoy a little music. When we have had our coffee you shall play to me.'

The piano, an excellent instrument, stood at one end of the drawing-room; Jemima, in her dull brown dress, sat down and ran her hands lightly over its keys. She hadn't had a chance to play for months and it would be a heavenly change from cribbage. 'What would you like, Lady Manderly?' She asked.

'Delius, Debussy, Schubert . . . Can you manage any of those?' The old lady's tone implied that she very much doubted it.

Jemima didn't answer; she was by no means a brilliant pianist, but she played with a good deal of feeling. 'The Walk to the Paradise Garden', while by no means technically perfect, was a delight to listen to. She scarcely heard Lady Manderly's 'Very nice,' uttered in rather surprised tones, before going on to 'A Song of Summer', and then 'Eine Kleine Nachtmusik.' Here she did pause, sitting with her hands quietly in her lap waiting to hear what Lady Manderly wanted next.

'Upon my soul,' declared that lady, 'you play very well, Jemima,' 'let me see—do you know the Cornish Rhapsody?'

Jemima played that too and then at her listener's request, the Vienna Dances, and, that finished: 'Quite delightful,' observed Lady Manderly. 'Who taught you to play so well?'

'My mother.' Jemima got up and closed the piano. 'I'm out of practice.'

'In that case, I have no objection to you playing each

day for an hour or so. Before dinner, while I'm dressing, would be a good time.'

'Thank you, Lady Manderly. Would you like to play bezique?'

'No, perhaps you would unpick my embroidery? I believe I've got the pattern wrong.'

Which was indeed true; Jemima had never seen such a muddle in all her life. It took her the rest of the evening while Lady Manderly, having a captive audience, reminisced about her youth. She required very little reply, which gave Jemima the leisure to think about Professor Cator—which she did, to the exclusion of everything else.

The next morning she asked if she might have her half day on Saturday, and since Lady Manderly was in a good frame of mind, she had little doubt that she would get it. To her surprise she was refused.

'Certainly not!' declared Lady Manderly. 'I will not play gooseberry to Alexander and Gloria, and I wish you to take your day off on some other day than Sunday. You may, of course, go to church if you like, but I want you to be available for the rest of the day.' She eyed Jemima's impassive face. 'I suggest you have a free day tomorrow instead, your half day can be fitted in at some other time.'

She really was an old tyrant, but there was nothing much she could do about it, decided Jemima. Probably Professor Cator and his Gloria would be so taken up with each other, they wouldn't bother if she were there or not.

She spent her free day in the town. She had several weeks' pay in her purse and the desire to buy a new dress was very great, but if she did, it would look very much as though she had done that because of the Professor and Gloria coming for the weekend and wanting to cut a dash. Which, of course, was quite true. Besides, she reminded herself, she was saving as much money as she could—an argument quickly dispelled when she saw exactly what she wanted in a tiny boutique off High Street: a chestnut brown jersey, very simple, with short sleeves and a little jacket. The skirt was pleated and calf-length; exactly suitable for her evenings with Lady Manderly. And the price was right too. After all, she hadn't had to pay for her room for three weeks now. She went inside, tried it on and bought it.

But she couldn't roam the town all day. She went to the films after a sketchy lunch and then had tea, making it last as long as possible. By the time she was outside again it was growing dark and she was tired. She retraced her steps to Church Lane and made her way round to the kitchen door. Only Mrs Spencer was in the kitchen and looked at her in surprise.

'Thought you had the day off, miss?' she exclaimed.

'Well, I have, but I've done my shopping and been to the cinema, now I want to write letters. Please don't tell Lady Manderly I'm back just yet—are there guests for dinner?'

Mrs Spencer nodded. 'Two ladies. I'll see that you get something to eat, miss.'

'You're a dear, Mrs Spencer. But don't bother to send anyone up. I'll come down and fetch a tray if you tell me what time.'

'Half past eight—it's sole bonne femme and caramel oranges.'

'Lovely, I'm going up the back stairs. You don't mind?'

In her own room she tried on the dress once more. It was every bit as nice as it had looked in the shop; she hung it away in the closet and settled down to her letter writing—an exaggerated letter to Dick, a long one to Shirley, describing her new dress, and then a clutch of brief letters full of nothings, to friends in Oxford. She was aware that they didn't much mind if they saw her again or not, but just for a little while longer they would keep up the polite fiction of writing to her, not really wanting to know what she was doing but feeling guiltily that they should do something about her.

She made it easy for them by writing that life was so busy and so varied in its happenings that letter-writing was becoming a luxury to be fitted in during her rare quiet moments. 'That'll let them off the hook,' she muttered, and went downstairs for her tray.

There wasn't much to do after that. Jemima washed her hair, had a long and far too hot bath and got into bed with the paperback she had bought that day, but presently she laid it down. Tomorrow Professor Cator would arrive; she couldn't wait to see him again, but at the same time she dreaded it. He would be cold and offhand and look at her with hard eyes, and she would be terrified of betraying her feelings. And there was Gloria, who would most likely make snide remarks about companions and wearing all the wrong clothes. Jemima registered a resolve to scrape her hair well back and wear the plainest of her skirts and jumpers, and since the brown dress was by far the dullest of her evening attire she would wear that. Thus heartened by this entirely feminine point of view, she turned out the light, had a good cry, and went to sleep.

She was out with Coco when they arrived just before lunch the next day. The Rolls was standing before the door when she arrived back. Mrs Spencer answered her ring, looking put out.

'Sorry to have brought you all this way,' said Jemima hastily.

'Oh, it ain't you, miss—it's that Miss Egerton, says her room's too cold and not enough lighting and wants a bathroom to herself. Which can't be done, as you well know; my lady has her own, an' we've got one to ourselves, but the other two 'as to do for guests in the 'ouse.'

'It's only for a weekend, Mrs Spencer,' said Jemima placatingly. 'And I'll take care not to get in Miss Egerton's way! Where's Lady Manderly?'

'In the drawing-room with Professor Cator and Miss Egerton. She said you were to go down to lunch when you came in.'

Jemima nodded resignedly, handed over Coco and went upstairs, where she brushed her hair into a severe style, wasted no time upon her face at all, and went downstairs again.

They were sitting round the fire, drinks in their hands and looking, she thought with surprise, uncommonly bored with each other. The Professor saw her first and got to his feet with a polite: 'Hullo, Jemima.' Lady Manderly turned her head regally. 'There you are, Jemima—too late for a drink.' While Gloria didn't look round.

Professor Cator appeared not to have heard his aunt; he poured sherry and brought it over to where Jemima had seated herself, a little way from the fire.

'Plenty of time,' he observed easily. 'There's no hurry, is there? Nothing on this afternoon.'

'No, Alexander, I daresay you and Gloria have plans of your own.'

'Nothing special—the theatre this evening, of course. Are you quite sure you won't come with us?'

'Positive, Alexander. We will dine early, though.'

'Oh, God,' said Gloria, 'that means I have to start

dressing at some unearthly hour, I suppose.' She sat up and looked at Jemima. 'Sometimes I wish I were a paid companion with a plain face and no clothes.'

'If that's meant to be a joke, I don't find it funny,' said the Professor icily. 'I've often thought that a good day's work would be of great benefit to you.'

Gloria tossed off the rest of her drink. 'I wouldn't know how,' she stated simply, and smiled angelically at him. 'I don't mean to be rude,' she explained to Jemima. 'I have this awful habit of saying exactly what I think.' She laughed gently. 'No one seems to mind.'

Jemima didn't say anything at all. Resentment was choking her and the thought of the next hour was enough to make her scream. She prayed she would get through it without turning on the girl and telling her just what she thought of her. She swallowed the rest of her sherry and looked out of the window. A burst of angry tears would have been a great comfort to her, but this was neither the time nor the place. Lady Manderly, obedient to Mrs Spencer's voice assuring her that lunch was on the table, got to her feet and led the way to the dining-room.

Contrary to her expectations, Jemima found that the meal wasn't the ordeal she had expected, largely because Professor Cator took the conversation into his own hands, allowing his aunt no more than an odd remark or two, and Gloria almost none at all. He addressed most of his conversation to the table at large, but was careful to include Jemima in it, and since he chose to carry on at some length about Shakespeare and his works, and it was obvious that Gloria wasn't in the least interested, she found herself responding warmly, a nice colour in her cheeks and her eyes sparkling with interest. Just for the moment she had forgotten that she loved him; that he disliked her, and that now she only knew that she was enjoying herself, that it was wonderful to talk to someone who was interested in the same things as she was herself.

It was Gloria who brought her down to earth. 'Can we change the subject?' she asked plaintively. 'It's bad enough that I've got to go to this beastly play this evening without having to have it rammed down my throat all day as well!'

Professor Cator looked at her thoughtfully. 'So sorry,' he said blandly, 'we got carried away.' He smiled at Gloria and at his aunt, who bowed her head graciously and declared that she had found the topic interesting enough. 'Although I know little enough about it, unlike my companion,' she added. 'We will excuse you, Jemima, there are those letters to see to; if you'll have them ready, I'll sign them and you can post them when you go out with Coco.'

'I didn't know you typed,' observed the Professor idly.

'I don't.' Jemima got up from the table and slipped away, to shut herself in the small sitting-room and write replies to Lady Manderly's various invitations in her neat hand, trying not to hear the laughter coming from the drawing-room.

She wore the brown dress again that evening, with her hair well dragged back, and got a sour satisfaction from Gloria's appearance: sapphire blue velvet of a devastatingly simple cut and some outrageously chunky jewellery which looked exactly right with it. As Jemima went into the drawing-room Gloria looked her up and down. 'Hullo, Jemima, still a brown mouse? And what in heaven's name have you done to your hair?' She laughed a little and shrugged gracefully. 'Oh, well, I suppose clever girls don't need to bother with themselves. Thank God I'm not clever . . .'

She broke off as Lady Manderly and her nephew

came into the room together and she crossed the room to tuck an arm into the Professor's. 'Don't I look nice?' she wanted to know. 'I think I'm going to enjoy myself after all.'

He answered her rather absently, his frowning gaze on Jemima. Gloria saw that. 'And don't stare at poor Jemima, just because she isn't wearing a pretty dress—there, now you've made her blush!'

Hateful creature, thought Jemima, needling me and knowing I can't do a thing about it.

But Gloria knew when to stop; nothing could have been friendlier than her manner towards Jemima during dinner, and outwardly at least, the meal was pleasant enough.

Lady Manderly was strangely silent after they had gone. She and Jemima had an hour of cribbage, then she got up from the card table and sat down, very upright, in her chair. And for once she was polite.

'I should like you to play to me,' she stated. 'I feel a little restless this evening, some music may calm me. Be good enough to lift Coco on to my knee and ask Mrs Spencer to bring a tray of coffee.'

And when this was done and Jemima had poured coffee for them both she was bidden to sit down and drink hers before going to the piano.

'We shall be leaving here shortly,' observed Lady Manderly. 'There's a good deal to see to before Christmas.'

It was the opportunity Jemima had been looking for. 'When Professor Cator first told me about the visit you intended to make here, I mentioned that I'd thought of leaving before Christmas. You see, Lady Manderly, I have to train for something or other—shorthand and typing for an office job, some sort of social work, nursing ... I haven't decided which I shall do, but I must start soon . . .'

'You dislike being my companion? You're not happy?' Lady Manderly sounded as though she couldn't believe her ears.

'I'm very happy, thank you, and I certainly don't dislike working for you, Lady Manderly, but you must see that sooner or later I must do something else—I'm twenty-seven, if I don't get married, and that isn't likely, I have thirty or so years ahead of me, and I have to do something worthwhile with them, build up a career if I can. I know I've left it rather late, but that's all the more reason to get started.'

'But you'll stay until I return to London?' Lady Manderly passed her cup for more coffee. 'I have your word on that?'

'Certainly, Lady Manderly.'

'Good. You may go to the piano now—I should like Chopin, I think, and perhaps a little Schubert.'

So Jemima sat down to play, the soft light from a table lamp shining on her, turning her quiet face and plump person into something very pleasing to the eye. 'Restful,' murmured Lady Manderly, and didn't mean the music.

Jemima played Chopin and thought about Alexander Cator. He would be sitting in one of the best seats, naturally, and Gloria would have tucked an exquisitly kept hand into his. The play was *All's Well that Ends Well*, very appropriate for the pair of them, she supposed, and what with the knowledge of her own hidden love, and the thought of a future empty of the Professor and the wistful Chopin Nocturne she was playing, she was hard put to it not to burst into tears.

She came to the end of it and dropped her hands into her lap, but Lady Manderly said at once: 'Go on, go on, let's have Schubert now.'

So Jemima played on, presently soothed just as much

as her listener. She went from Schubert to Handel and then, her good sense asserting itself once more and feeling a shade militant, she started on Beethoven. Her technique left much to be desired, but she played with a good deal of fire and feeling, which was probably why she didn't hear the return of Gloria and the Professor. And Lady Manderly didn't hear them either; she was sleeping, still sitting bolt upright, snoring faintly.

Beethoven dealt with, Jemima started on Delius. The 'Walk to the Paradise Garden' suited her mood, which, no longer bolstered up by Beethoven's rolling chords, had become decidedly sad. She didn't hear the door open; the Professor stood there listening to her for quite a few minutes before she finished and turned on her stool to speak to Lady Manderly.

Jemima closed the lid and got up at once, and he strolled over to her, casting a smiling glance at his sleeping aunt as he did so.

'The play was excellent, but I believe I should have enjoyed myself even better if I'd stayed here and listened to you playing. You're a woman of parts, Jemima.'

'Lady Manderly likes me to play to her sometimes, but as she's asleep now I'll fetch Pooley.' She skipped past him, rather in the manner of someone avoiding a dangerous whirlpool. 'I'll say goodnight, Professor Cator.'

She hadn't been quite quick enough; he caught her arm, quite gently, and drew her back. 'I'll say goodnight too,' he said softly, and kissed her. It was a pity that he added as he let her go: 'That brown dress suits you.' It reminded her how dowdy she must look after Gloria's glowing velvet and reminded her who she was, too. She went out of the room without a word.

She didn't even look at him, and if Lady Manderly had woken up and seen it all, she didn't care two pins.

Probably she would be sacked the next morning, like Victorian governesses caught with the son of the house. She giggled as she went up stairs, but the giggle turned into a sob.

CHAPTER SEVEN

Jemima was quite out in her guessing. She went down to breakfast in the morning to find Lady Manderly and her nephew already at the table, and by the way they looked at her as she went in, talking about her too. Gloria, of course, was having her breakfast in bed. Jemima took the chair the Professor had politely set for her, wished them both good morning and poured herself some coffee. The air of innocence upon Lady Manderly's face, while quite out of place, was highly suspicious. Jemima buttered toast, added marmalade and waited quietly.

She had taken the first bite when Lady Manderly spoke. 'I've decided to go to Scotland for a couple of weeks,' she observed weightily. 'I have a small lodge there—it belonged to my husband, he was accustomed to spend August and September there each year. In the highlands on the Morar coast. We'll fly to Glasgow, take the train to Oban and hire a car to take us the rest of the way.'

Jemima put down her toast. 'But, Lady Manderly, I understood that we were returning to London within the next week or so . . .'

'I have changed my mind,' said Lady Manderly in regal tones. 'Unless you have a new post waiting for you, I can see no reason why you shouldn't accompany me. I need you.'

Jemima took a quick peep at the Professor. He was eating his eggs and bacon with an inscrutable face and listening to every word.

'I have a feeling that I'm being got at,' she said clearly.

Lady Manderly's face became richly purple, but before she could speak Professor Cator said smoothly: 'Now why should you think that, Jemima? You've told me that you have no job to go to.' He exchanged a lightning glance with his aunt. 'I believe the intention is for my aunt to leave for Arisaig within the next day or so; so that you'll still return to London a mere few days later.'

'But surely the weather . . .' began Jemima weakly. 'I mean, it's winter, isn't it, wherever we're going?'

'The west coast of the Highlands,' he told her blandly, 'is known for its mild climate. And the lodge is very comfortable.'

She gave him a look and addressed herself to Lady Manderly.

'I had intended to put an advertisement in one of the London papers, Lady Manderly . . .' She stopped, remembering that she had declared her intention of training for something or other; she had given it as the reason for leaving. She reddened, but neither of her companions appeared to have noticed. Professor Cator, buttering a roll, looked up briefly to say:

'If you like to write it out, I'll see that it goes into one of the evening papers and that any replies are sent on to you.'

Jemima had her mouth open to refuse and then, in the face of his blandly smiling countenance, closed it again. She loved him with her whole heart, but just at that moment she would willingly have boxed his ears. After a few moments she remarked matter-of-factly:

'Well, I really don't see how I can go . . . I haven't any warm clothing with me, only some sweaters and a raincoat.'

It was Lady Manderly who spoke this time. 'That is quickly arranged. I have only to telephone to Belling and ask him to go to your lodgings and collect anything you may need.'

Jemima looked doubtful. 'I don't suppose it would get here in time—the post, you know.'

'There's some sort of urgent delivery, I believe; a couple of days should suffice.' The Professor's voice was almost placid, but she thought she heard laughter in it.

She looked at Lady Manderly and was surprised to see her looking anxious. Perhaps the old lady really did want her to go, perhaps she had some sentimental reason for going to the lodge at all the wrong time in the year. She said slowly: 'Very well, Lady Manderly, I'll come with you.'

Lady Manderly inclined her head in regal thanks. 'We will leave here in three days' time. Be good enough to have a list of the things you require as soon as possible after breakfast. Perhaps it would be as well if you spoke to Belling yourself.'

Jemima turned to her neglected breakfast. 'Yes, Lady Manderly.' She buttered toast with a steady hand, aware of excitement. It would be interesting to see the Highlands in early winter; at the same time it would mean that Professor Cator would be even farther away. Not that distance made any difference, she reminded herself. However near they were to each other he would never notice her as a person—a girl— she had to admit, with nothing to notice about her, anyway.

His voice interrupted her thoughts. 'If I might suggest, Aunt, it would be far easier if you were to drive up from Glasgow. There are plenty of firms who'll send a car and driver to meet you at the airport.'

'A good idea, Alexander. I shall do that; Jemima shall see to it . . .'

'No need,' his voice was careless, 'I can arrange it for you.' He handed Jemima his cup for more coffee. 'Are we going to church?'

'Naturally we all go,' stated Lady Manderly. 'If you've finished your breakfast, Jemima, be good enough to go to Gloria's room and remind her that we leave the house at half past ten.'

Gloria wasn't even eating her breakfast; the tray on the table by her bed was untouched, while she lay back reading a magazine.

She greeted Jemima with a careless, 'Hullo. What do you want?'

'Nothing, but I have a message from Lady Manderly—that we all leave the house at half past ten for church.'

'You may, I shan't. It's nine o'clock already and I haven't had breakfast yet, and I take hours to dress. Tell her I'm prostrate with a headache.'

'You'd have heaps of time if you had your breakfast now and got up straight away.'

Gloria put down her magazine. 'Don't be silly,' she begged languidly, 'I shall do exactly what I like.'

Jemima went downstairs again, uncertain what to do. It was a pity that she met both Lady Manderly and her nephew in the hall.

'Is she up?' he wanted to know.

'Well, no—not quite.' Jemima addressed herself to the old lady. 'Gloria wondered if you'd mind very much if she doesn't come to church . . .'

She watched Lady Manderly's cheeks empurple; one

day the old lady would have a stroke or something.

'Leave this to me.' Professor Cator's voice was brisk;
he had disappeared up the stairs as he had spoken, and
a moment later they heard a door open and close with
a snap. Lady Manderly said almost tearfully: 'The
girl's impossible—so why can't he see that? But perhaps he does . . .' She was so obviously talking to herself that Jemima didn't answer, but opened the sitting-
room door, and when they were inside, closed it again
firmly. She longed wholeheartedly to know what was
going on upstairs, but no one was going to accuse her
of eavesdropping. She said calmly: 'I'll make that list,
shall I? Is there time to phone Belling before we go to
church? Would you like me to make a list for you at
the same time, Lady Manderly?'

The old lady looked at the closed door and just for a
moment Jemima thought she was going to open it and
stand in the hall in the hope of hearing what was happening upstairs, but she went and sat in her usual chair.
'Yes, you may make a list of things I shall need, and
one for yourself; Belling shall see to them at once.'

The next half hour was taken up with writing. Lady
Manderly changed her mind at least twice while Jemima
sat patiently, one ear tuned to the silence outside the
room. She had the final lists ready by the time the
door opened and the Professor joined them. It was
tiresome of him not to say anything; he sat down and
unfolded the first of the Sunday papers and she went
away to telephone to Belling—a lengthy business, since
she judged it wise to make him read it all back to her.
And when she had finished with him, she phoned
Shirley. The phone was behind the post office counter
and she was rather afraid that Shirley might not hear it
in the flat above; it was Sunday and she enjoyed what
she called a good lie-in then, but she was in luck.

Shirley's cheerful cockney voice answered after a short interval, wanting to know who it was. Jemima explained:

'And Belling will come along quite soon,' she pointed out, 'if you wouldn't mind looking in my trunk for the things on the list he's got with him. And I'll be back soon now—I think Lady Manderly only wants to stay in Scotland for a week or ten days.' She didn't mention that she intended to leave her employer; by the time she got back, with luck, there would be some answers to her advertisement. She hung up finally and went back to the sitting-room to tell Lady Manderly that Belling would get one of the maids to start the necessary packing up at once, and then retired to her own room, where she wrote out an advertisement. It took several attempts to get it quite right, but in the end she was satisfied, and since it was almost time to leave for church, she put on her jacket and a small felt hat, picked up gloves and handbag and went downstairs.

Lady Manderly, in mink and fine broadcloth, was sitting in her chair again, her nephew was still reading. Jemima crossed the room and addressed the back of the *Sunday Times*. 'I've written the advertisement,' she told him to his unseen face. 'If you would be good enough to put it in the evening paper, and perhaps the *Daily Telegraph*, and if you'll let me know how much . . .'

He put out a hand and took the paper she offered him. 'I'll see to it and let you know the cost.'

The door opened and his uninterested gaze swept over her shoulder as Gloria came into the room. It was clearly obvious that she was in a bad temper, for her lovely mouth was turned down at its corners, making it thin and ugly. She ignored everyone but stood in the middle of the room, one hand on a hip, waiting for someone to speak, which gave Jemima ample opportunity to take in the short fur jacket, elegant shirt and still more elegant boots. A little fur cap crowned her golden head and she was swinging a tan leather handbag and gloves from one hand. She looked perfectly gorgeous, thought Jemima, and moved away from the window because the contrast was too awful for words.

'We might as well go,' observed the Professor calmly; Jemima wondered how he could look at Gloria so coolly when she was so beautiful. Perhaps he was used to her by now. He certainly betrayed no annoyance when she declared that she would sit in the back of the car with Lady Manderly. Jemima got in beside him, feeling a tearing excitement because she was actually so close to him. It made her pale, which hardly added to her looks.

And once in church, Lady Manderly led the way down the aisle and took her place in a pew under the pulpit, and after a glance at the Professor Gloria followed her. But he made no move, only pushed Jemima gently in her back so that she sat reluctantly beside Gloria. That left the last seat for the Professor. Pig in the middle, thought Jemima, getting on to her knees.

She sang the hymns in an unselfconscious treble, very sweet but not very powerful, but it wouldn't have mattered if her voice had been twice as strong, for Professor Cator had a rich bass which boomed out above her head, effectively drowning any voice within yards. Gloria didn't sing at all; she stood and sat and knelt like a puppet and Jemima could feel the waves of rage emitting from her elegant person. Peeping sideways at the Professor's placid face, she deplored his craftiness in urging her to sit next to Gloria. Thank heaven she would have to take Coco for her walk directly after they got back from church; perhaps they would settle their differences in the meantime. It seemed wicked to think such thoughts in church, but she couldn't help wishing they would quarrel so hard that Gloria would disappear out of his life for ever. She sat, looking attentively at the vicar in his pulpit, preaching what was probably an excellent sermon, and allowed herself to dream a little. She would, in some unexplained way, become beautiful overnight, the plumpness which she deplored would have disappeared and her conversation would be amusing and witty, so that the Professor would hang on her every word and fall in love with her and before she agreed to marry him she would tell him that he would have to mend his ways ... that wasn't true, she would marry him, faults and all; after all, he had been kind and gentle with the cat. She smiled a little remembering it, unaware that he was watching her, sitting sideways in the pew. She loved him very much and there was absolutely nothing she could do about it. Her gentle mouth trembled a little and the smile faded ...

'And now to God the Father ...' intoned the vicar, and she got to her feet with everyone else, feeling childishly guilty because she hadn't heard one word of the sermon.

Back at the house at Lady Manderly's command, she went to fetch Coco and left by the back door, only to find Professor Cator stalking along the path to meet her.

'You've had no coffee,' he pointed out.

'Oh, that's all right,' she told him pleasantly. 'Mrs Spencer will give me a cup when we get back.'

'You're not a servant!'

She gave him a clear look from her lovely eyes. 'Yes, I am, Professor.'

She walked past him, but he turned and caught up with her. 'One other thing,' he observed. 'Why were you smiling in church, and then you looked as though you were going to cry?'

She stared up at him, a slow blush creeping over her cheeks. 'I've no idea,' she said breathlessly. 'And now I really must go or we shan't be back in time for lunch.'

He stood aside without another word, and she went down the path and out of the gate.

When she entered the drawing-room an hour later it was to find Lady Manderly sitting in her chair, radiating disapproval, Gloria looking sulky and the Professor looking positively thunderous. He offered her sherry and she accepted, and made an effort to lighten the atmosphere. 'It's getting much colder,' she offered. 'I wonder if we're going to have a hard winter?'

Gloria turned her back, walking across the room and pouring herself another gin and tonic. The Professor's eyes followed her and he looked as though he was going to speak. But he didn't, it was Lady Manderly who gave Jemima an unexpected look of approval and answered her poor effort at conversation.

'I think that may be so, Jemima. Personally I rather like the winter. Stratford is pleasant out of season, I shall be sorry to leave here, but I have a strong wish to visit the Lodge.' She added in a voice that dared her listener to agree: 'I am, after all, an old woman with not many years more left to me.'

Jemima sought for a suitable answer to this and was relieved when the Professor, his eyes still on Gloria, said forcefully: 'My dear Aunt, you're good for another twenty years, and you know it.'

This led, naturally enough, to a monologue on Lady Manderly's part, describing her various illnesses, which lasted well into lunch and was kept going by astute remarks from her nephew. Jemima was silent for most of the meal, but only because there was no need to talk, and Gloria was silent because she was still hopping mad. When she did speak it was in an ugly voice which quite belied her lovely face; complaining that the food she was offered was quite unsuitable. 'It's so important to keep slim,' she said, and looked pointedly at Jemima. 'I'm a size ten and intend to remain so.' She smiled across the table. 'I'm sure you're a fourteen, Jemima?'

'Twelve.' Jemima helped herself to another portion of trifle and ate it with pleasure.

'It must be a bit of a squeeze . . .'

'Be quiet, Gloria!' said the Professor suddenly.

Jemima finished her trifle calmly, agreed with equally calm tones to write a letter on Lady Manderly's behalf and post it when she went out with Coco, drank her coffee in a rather strained atmosphere, and escaped. The Professor was an annoying, arrogant man; she loved him so much that all she wanted was to see him happy, even if it meant him marrying Gloria, but she would have given five years of her life to have saved him from what she fully expected would be a most unpleasant drive back to London.

They had gone by the time she got back with Coco. Lady Manderly was sitting in the drawing-room making an absolute hash of her embroidery. Jemima took it from her without a word, did some unpicking, threaded some silks and handed it back, then asked a few pertinent questions about Scotland.

'I've told Pooley to start packing,' observed her companion. 'I shall of course need the thicker dresses and coats which Belling is sending. If you wish, you may pack whatever you don't need to take with you, and a case can be sent back to London from here. We need very little.'

Lady Manderly's idea of very little meant three large suitcases, a jewel box and an overnight bag. Jemima ruthlessly discarded most of her clothes, added the slacks and skirt and woollies Shirley had sent via Belling, and declared herself ready. At the last minute she had packed the new dress; Lady Manderly had told her that she didn't stand on ceremony when she was staying at the lodge, but Jemima thought it a good idea to play safe. And it was a pity not to wear the dress even if there was no one to see it. No one being Alexander Cator, of course.

The journey went smoothly. Lady Manderly was conveyed, giving orders and countermanding them with the next breath, from her house to the airport and from the plane to the waiting hired car—a quite arduous task for Jemima and Pooley, who were only too glad to get into the car with her, and allow themselves to be driven the last hundred and fifty odd miles. They stopped for refreshment at the hotel in Ardlui, and Jemima took Coco for a brisk walk along the shore of Loch Lomand. She would have liked to have lingered there, but Lady Manderly was impatient to get to the lodge and they drove on, taking the road to Fort William and then turning west on to the A830 to Mallaig. Arisaig was some miles short of that town, and lay at the head of Loch nan Ceall, and Jemima was enchanted with the magnificent scenery. It was a small place with a bustling harbour, full, her companion told her, in the summer months with pleasure yachts and cruisers. Now it was comparatively quiet, with only the fishing boats to be seen and very few people about in the dull grey of late afternoon.

They went through the village and turned off the road into a lane winding uphill, and presently turned into an open gateway, still going uphill through closely packed trees. The lodge stood in a small circle of rough grass with trees all round it; a fair sized stone house with a slate roof, small square windows and a great many gables. If it hadn't been for the lights streaming from the downstairs windows, it might have appeared unwelcoming.

The front door was opened as the car came to a halt and a short sandy-haired woman came out to greet them, addressing them in a cheerful cockney voice.

'Everything's ready for you, my lady,' she offered. 'My old man's down in the village, but e'll be back in no time. 'E's fixed for the driver to stay the night there. You'll be wanting yer dinner, no doubt.'

'In half an hour, Martha. I'll go to my room, then take Miss Mason to hers—Pooley will have her usual room, I suppose?'

'S' right, my lady.' Martha's shrewd eyes rested for a moment on Jemima, who smiled as she turned away to pay the driver and ask him to bring in the luggage. Lady Manderly was already in the hall when she called back:

'Before you come in, Jemima, you'd better take Coco for a little run.'

So it was ten minutes or more before Jemima followed Martha up the stairs to the landing above and into a pleasant room down a short passage.

'The bathroom's next door, miss. Me and Angus 'ave a room at the back of the 'ouse—we sleep in, but we spend Saturday night and all day Sunday with our daughter—she's married to a chap in Mallaig.' She paused in the doorway. 'Lady Manderly, she 'asn't never brought her companions 'ere before.'

Jemima was looking out of the window at the en-circling trees. 'No? Perhaps she preferred to be alone. Do I call you Martha, or or would you rather I used your married name?'

'Martha'll do, miss. I must say it's a rum time of year to come up 'ere. Lovely autumn we've 'ad, but the weather's going to worsen, so Angus says, and 'e's mostly right.'

Jemima undid her case and began to take out her clothes. 'I do hope not. It looks lovely, and the views are breathtaking.'

Martha grinned. 'Not 'alf they aren't when it's been snowing for a day or two!' She turned away. 'I'll leave you to unpack, miss. My lady's at the front of the 'ouse—the double doors on the landing. Pooley's near us at the back. There's a girl comes up to 'elp morn-ings, but most of the bedrooms are kept closed, so there's not that much to do.'

Left to herself, Jemima hung her things in the vast old-fashioned wardrobe, did her hair and her face, and went along to Lady Manderly's room.

There was little for her to do there. Pooley was un-packing and Lady Manderly was sitting in a comfort-able chair by the open fire. As soon as she saw Jemima she said without preamble: 'Go and telephone Alexander and tell him we've arrived safely, and then wait for me in the sitting-room.'

It wasn't until Jemima was lifting the receiver that she remembered she had no idea of the Professor's number. She was by no means the perfect companion, she thought, then caught sight of the address book on the table.

A man answered—an elderly voice, very polite. No, the Professor was out, but a message would be delivered when he returned. She rang off, her head full of colourful pictures of Alexander Cator and Gloria having a splendid evening together in one of the more fashionable night clubs in London. If she had stopped to think she would have realised that the Professor was hardly the sort to frequent night spots, but love was causing her to have some peculiar ideas.

While she waited for Lady Manderly, she looked around her. The sitting-room was pleasant enough, although it wore the air of not having been used lately, and when she peeped into the dining-room that looked much the same, although the table, laid with a fine linen cloth and set with silver and glass, looked inviting. There was a third door; a smaller room, a mixture of library and study, leading to a closed verandah. The kitchen, she supposed, was through the baize door beside the stairs, and the door behind the sitting-room opened into a quite large room with a piano at one end and a billiard table at its centre. The whole place was comfortably furnished and lacked none of the comforts; it might be miles from anywhere, but it was well maintained. It struck her that it was a little extravagant to maintain a house of this size when it was occupied for only a couple of weeks each year, but perhaps other members of Lady Manderly's family spent their holidays there too. Jemima went back to the sitting-room and stood looking out of the window into the dark evening until Lady Manderly joined her.

Over dinner Jemima learned that even in the remote Highlands, her duties would be as manifold as before. For one thing, few of Lady Manderly's friends lived within calling distance and almost all of those had gone back to London, which meant that there would be little to distract her. Jemima, she was informed, was to arrange a hire car in the morning, and drive her em-

ployer around the surrounding countryside. She was
also warned that at least a hundred Christmas cards
would need to have their envelopes addressed and last,
but not least, a list of necessary Christmas presents
must be made. 'And you can, of course, play to me in
the evenings,' added Lady Manderly. 'I am rarely in
the mood for television. When you have arranged for
the car, we will drive to Mallaig, there is a good library
there, and I will select some books.'

To all of which Jemima agreed in her pleasant voice;
it was, after all, only a short stay and she was glad of
the money. She had spent very little since they had left
London; only the new dress and dull things like stamps
and toothpaste. She reminded herself that every penny
would count once she got back which made her remember her advertisement; perhaps there would be
some letters to answer before they left Arisaig—that
was if Professor Cator had remembered to send her
advertisement to the papers.

There was frost on the ground when she got up the
next morning. She put on slacks and a thick sweater
and went down to the kitchen, where she found Martha
sitting at the table drinking tea. She poured another
cup for Jemima. 'You're an early bird, miss, couldn't
you sleep?'

'Very well, thank you. I came down to see you,
Martha. Lady Manderly has her breakfast in bed and I
don't know about me . . .'

'You can 'ave it on a tray in the dining-room, miss.'

'Well, if you don't mind, I'd much rather have it
here with you—would you and your husband and
Pooley object?'

Martha gave her an approving look. 'Lor' luv you,
no, miss. Glad ter 'ave yer company. We eat at half
past eight.'

'That's fine. Lady Manderly likes me to go to her about nine o'clock, so I'll have time to take Coco for a quick run round the garden before breakfast.'

The day unfolded itself slowly. A car was hired, delivered before lunch and tried out by Jemima. The first batch of cards was written and although no list was made, Lady Manderly spent a good part of the morning discussing what she should buy for the various members of her family, and how cheaply it could be done. For someone who denied herself nothing, she was remarkably mean when it came to giving anything away. But she seemed to be enjoying herself, telephoning her friends, arranging menus, browbeating poor Pooley; Jemima, at the end of the day, went thankfully enough to her bed. What with writing envelopes until she had cramp, walking Coco morning and afternoon in a cold mist which had obscured everything around her, and then playing cribbage for hours after dinner, she was worn out. But tomorrow, she promised herself, it would be better. For one thing they were to drive to Mallaig and for another, Lady Manderly had told her that provided nothing happened to make her change her mind, Jemima might have a free afternoon.

Mallaig was large compared with Arisaig. It had two hotels for a start, although one of them was closed for the winter, and several good shops. Jemima drove the seven miles there, along the narrow road with its passing places and the railway running close by, and since the mist had gone there was plenty to see while Lady Manderly graciously held forth about the three islands at the entrance to the Loch, Rum, Eigg and Muck. Lovely names, thought Jemima. Shirley would never believe her when she wrote and told her.

She parked the car and escorted Lady Manderly from one shop to the next, posted the cards which were written and then accompanied her to a bookshop where she took the opportunity of buying herself a couple of paper backs while her employer, sitting grandly in a chair, chose an armful of books and magazines. Far too many to carry; Jemima had to go and fetch the car and leave it outside the shop while the proprietor loaded everything into the boot.

They got back in time for lunch and they were just finishing that meal when Alexander Cator telephoned. Jemima answered it, and struck dumb by the sound of his voice, had nothing to say for herself, so that he repeated his request to speak to his aunt with a testiness which brought her out of her daydream. She still didn't say anything, but put the receiver down and fetched Lady Manderly, then went away to find Coco for her walk. She should have been prepared for his telephoning; he must find her a stupid girl. Next time she would be coolly brisk.

She wore the new dress that evening. It seemed a pity to leave it hanging in the cupboard, and just putting it on made her feel a lot better. Of course it was still brown like the other one, but it was a pretty brown this time and it suited her. Lady Manderly, in black crêpe-de-chine and pearls, approved of it. 'You have good taste,' she allowed. 'Your clothes are rather dull, but then of course you have to buy things which will wear well, but I must admit that you make the most of them.' She got up from the dinner table. 'I shall read this evening and you shall play to me.'

Well, it was a whole lot better than playing cribbage! Jemima went from Ravel, to Bach, *My Fair Lady* to *Bitter Sweet* and then back to Ravel and finally to Delius.

'That's very sad,' observed her listener as she finished and sat quietly with her hands folded in her lap. 'Do you feel sad, Jemima?'

It was so unexpected a question coming from Lady Manderly, who had never expressed any interest in her before, that Jemima couldn't think of a ready answer. Presently she said: 'Well, not exactly, sad, Lady Manderly, I'm very happy and contented and I'm looking forward to learning something useful when we get back to London. Just sometimes I remember my home . . .'

'You are in love, perhaps?'

Jemima looked down at her hands and willed herself not to blush. 'That would hardly fit into my life at present, Lady Manderly. Would you like me to continue playing?'

Her companion shot her a peevish look. 'You're sometimes too ready with your tongue, Jemima. I enjoy offering advice to those who need it. But you know your own business best, of course.' Her voice was as peevish as her look.

'You're very kind, Lady Manderly, but I have no need of advice, thank you.'

Lady Manderly snorted. 'You prefer to eat your heart out, do you? I'll say no more. Fetch Pooley for me, will you? I shall go to bed, and I suggest that you do the same.'

Jemima got to her feet. 'Goodnight, Lady Manderly—I'll get Pooley at once.'

Sitting up in bed later, she discovered that she wasn't at all sleepy. She should have been, because she had spent the afternoon walking the two miles or so to Arisaig, and although the hotel was empty of guests, they obligingly gave her tea after she had walked along the sands to the north of the village.

It had been cold and very beautiful, with a stormy sea and a biting wind and flurries of icy rain, but she

had enjoyed every minute of it. She had even enjoyed
the walk back to the lodge, uphill all the way. Next
week, she promised herself, when she had her half day,
she would explore further. It was a pity that Lady
Manderly liked her to have her day off on Sundays,
because there was little to do on that day especially at
this time of year.

She lay back in her comfortable bed, her forgotten
book on the counterpane, planning her future, although she could do little about it at the moment, but
once there were some replies to her advert . . . If there
were any.

There were, the very next morning. Three, and none
of them sounded promising. She had anticipated a
temporary post, so that she could decide what she
intended to do. She would have to have a career and
the easiest way would be to learn shorthand and typing.
If she could arrange to go to night school for three
months she might get a small job to start with and
work up from there. Her heart wasn't in it, though; to
sit at a desk all day seemed a dull way in which to earn
a living, but it could lead to better things. She re-read
the letters. The first one wanted someone to care for
the granny of the family, blind, and if she read cor-
rectly between the lines, difficult. Daughter and son-
in-law worked all day, and there were three children at
day school. The second was for a strong young woman
to care for a disabled boy; so few details were given
that Jemima put it back in its envelope and turned to
the third one. The worst of the lot; someone to house-
keep for an old married couple living in the granny
annexe of a house in Hampstead, and also expected to
help in the main house, do the shopping and take and
fetch the children to and from school. None of them
would do, she decided unhappily; unless something

more suitable turned up, she would have to go back to Mrs Adams and live on her savings until she could find a job—any job. She was making things hard for herself, she realised that; Lady Manderly would keep her on if she asked her, but she couldn't bear to stay, not with the chance of seeing Alexander Cator several times a week. Blow the man, said Jemima forcefully, and went downstairs to sit with Lady Manderly and read the daily papers to her.

They went to Fort William in the afternoon. On the road, narrow to begin with, but widening as they approached the town, and Jemima was able to glance around at the scenery—mountains and yet more mountains and thick forest. And the town was charming; bustling and cheerful, the shops already decked with decorations for Christmas. She parked the car and accompanied Lady Manderly on a present-finding excursion which lasted until the afternoon began to darken.

'We'd better have tea,' observed Lady Manderly grudgingly. She led the way into a tea-shop and ordered tea and scones and bade Jemima check her list. Very few presents had been bought: Jemima thought privately that it would be a far better idea if her employer waited until she got back to London and then spent an hour or so in Harrods. She had an account there, so she wouldn't have the pain of parting with actual money from her purse—an opinion borne out presently by Lady Manderly declaring that she had no small change and would Jemima pay.

It was dark as they drove back and by the time they reached the lodge, the wind had freshened. 'I do believe it's going to snow,' observed Jemima as she collected parcels from the car and saw Lady Manderly into the house. And sure enough, by the time she had put the car away in the garage at the back of the lodge, the first soft flakes were floating down.

By the time they were sitting at dinner, it was snowing in real earnest, but when she mentioned this: 'The snow will cease by morning,' declared her companion in much the same tone of voice King Canute must have used when ordering the North Sea not to come any nearer. 'There's no need to get excited about a moderate fall of snow,' she pointed out in her usual hectoring manner. 'Martha and Angus have driven to Mallaig for the night, and they would never have gone if they had expected the snow to settle.'

Jemima thought privately that if she had been Martha and Angus with the prospect of snow stopping them from visiting their daughter, she would have gone while the going was good. But she didn't say so.

She spent the evening addressing more envelopes, for as her employer reminded her, she had done nothing to earn her keep all day.

CHAPTER EIGHT

JEMIMA slept soundly, to be wakened by Pooley with a cup of tea a good deal later than Martha usually brought it.

'Oh, miss,' said Pooley, with a face as long as a fiddle, 'the snow's awful, and we're all alone—Martha and Angus will never get back. What are we going to do?'

Jemima leapt out of bed and pulled back the curtains. It was snowing steadily, piling up into hills where there weren't any, with drifts covering the hedges and shrubs, the drive quite invisible, all unbelievably white and quite unrecognisable. She got back into bed and drank her tea.

'Well, I don't think we need to worry too much, do you? Even if we can't get far there's the telephone and the television . . .'

'I can't cook, miss,' said Pooley in a doomladen voice.

'I can. If you could manage the fires, I'll scout around the kitchen and get breakfast and get round to the shed by the garage—there's masses of coal there, and there's bound to be a shovel. The thing is to keep Lady Manderly cheerful.'

Pooley scurried off, and Jemima dressed and went down to the kitchen. Breakfast was easy—orange juice, toast, butter, marmalade and coffee, arranged on a delicate cloth upon a tray while Pooley took tea up to Lady Manderly. Jemima had it all ready by the time she came downstairs again, and then she set about getting a meal for themselves. There was less food in the fridge than she would have liked to see, but there was a small sack of oats, plenty of tea, not much bread and even less milk, although there were tins of things like pâté de fois gras and truffles and caviare. The fridge yielded some bacon, half a dozen eggs, a bowl of salad and some cream, and the deep freezer, beyond a couple of iron-hard chickens and some stewing steak, was empty. It seemed a funny way to run a house remote from even the nearest village shop, but Pooley solved the mystery when she came back. The stores at Arisaig delivered the week's groceries on Wednesday afternoons; she had heard the housekeeper phoning it through only the day before and saying that they were very low in supplies. And, Pooley pointed out, today was Wednesday. They stared at each other for a long minute. 'Oh, dear, oh dear!' sighed Jemima, and then:

'I hope you like porridge!'

'We'll have to make a plan,' Jemima pointed out over
their porridge. 'I mean, we'll have to keep the house
tidy and make the beds and see to the fires. The central
heating's oil-fired, isn't it? I hope the oil won't freeze—
I don't even know where it comes from . . . I'll go and
talk to Lady Manderly presently and explain that we'll
have quite a bit to do—thank heaven for the radio and
the telly!' She poured them both more tea. 'Let's go
round the store cupboards and see what there is. I
wonder how long this weather lasts?'

Pooley had no idea. 'What about Coco?' she asked.

'Oh, lord, I'd forgotten all about her.' Jemima got
up from the table. 'Look, I'm going to look for some
wellies and an old coat. I'll take Coco out—I'll have
to—and then we'll explore the kitchen thoroughly. I
wonder if Lady Manderly knows where Martha and
Angus are and if they're on the phone.'

There were both boots and thick cape with a hood
behind the back door. Jemima scooped up Coco under
one arm and opened the door, to be met with a flurry
of snow, almost blinding her. But she saw that it was
whirling past the door, piling up against the wall in
deep drifts; at least they would be able to get in and
out for the moment. She set Coco on to the snow. 'And
for heaven's sake be quick!' she begged the little dog.

Coco needed no urging. She bolted back through
the door when Jemima opened it and went to sit by the
Aga, which was warm, while Jemima took off the cape
and boots, tidied herself in front of the kitchen mirror,
and went upstairs to see Lady Manderly.

That lady, still snug in her bed, was disposed to
make light of the situation. 'You have Pooley to help
you,' she pointed out, 'two strong women—and no one
but myself to look after.'

Jemima stood her ground. 'I'm afraid we shall be busy this morning, Lady Manderly. We must clear the snow for a start, get in some coal, find some shovels, tidy the house, make the beds, cook the meals . . .'

Lady Manderly waved a dismissive hand. 'I can see that I am the one to suffer,' she said with selfconscious fortitude. 'Send Pooley to me and I'll dress. Presumably I'm not to have your services this morning, Jemima?'

'Well, it would help a bit if you could manage on your own, Lady Manderly,' observed Jemima forthrightly. 'This is quite a big house. I thought it might help a bit if we just had a fire in the sitting-room. I'm not sure where the coal is, for a start, and it's going to be difficult to get it indoors.'

Lady Manderly cast her eyes up to heaven. 'What a number of mountains you're making out of a few molehills! And I thought you to be such a sensible girl.'

'I am, that's why I'm suggesting that we just have one fire, Lady Manderly.' Jemima beat a retreat before Lady Manderly could answer.

Pooley was away a long time; Jemima had washed up the breakfast things, tidied the kitchen, Hoovered the hall, the sitting-room and as much of the stair carpet as she could reach, and rushed around with a duster before the maid appeared looking agitated.

'My lady wants chicken supreme for her dinner tonight,' she almost wailed. 'Whatever shall we do?' She would have wrung her hands, but Jemima, anxious to get the chores done, thrust a duster into them.

'Well, there is a chicken in the freezer—I'll get it out now—it's rather short notice, but that can't be helped. Lady Manderly shall have her chicken supreme. I've been going over the cupboards; there are plenty of jelly packets and tins of fruit, that'll do for a sweet. She can have an omelette for lunch.'

'What about us?' asked Pooley.

'Potatoes in their jackets and some cheese on top—we'll worry about dinner when we get to it.' Jemima glanced out of the window; the sky was a nasty dead grey, although it had stopped snowing. 'Look, will you whip round the bedrooms and make the beds, make up the fire and get the coffee? I'm going outside to see where everything is.'

'You'll catch your death of cold,' said Pooley mournfully. Not an ideal companion for an emergency, thought Jemima, taking off her apron and going to hunt among the garments hung haphazard on hooks by the kitchen door. She got into the boots again, selected a well worn anorak several sizes too big for her, added a disreputable old cloth cap and some wooly gloves, and pronounced herself ready.

Outside, with Pooley's unhappy voice begging her to be careful echoing through the shut door, she took stock of their surroundings. She knew the garage, of course, but she had never had occasion to look into the shed alongside it. Probably there would be a spade there, and that was the most urgent thing, and after that, to find the coal . . .

The snow was deep. By the time she had reached the shed it had seeped over the tops of her boots and was melting down into her feet. It was only as she reached for the handle of the shed door that she remembered that she hadn't thought about it being locked. It wasn't. She heaved a sigh of relief and began on the slow job of shifting the snow so that she could open it, muttering to herself the while. 'This is a man's job, but as usual there isn't one handy. If only Alexander were here!'

She felt a quite unexpected sob choke her, but she

swallowed it down, attacked the snow once more, and prised the door open. There was a spade inside and even better, a snow shovel, rather large and heavy, but it would do the job much faster. Perhaps she could get Pooley to help her. There was no coal, though. She dragged the spade and shovel outside and shut the door and started back to the house, to search the back wall for a likely door which might lead to coal. She found it presently, dug it free, and opened it. There was coal enough and stacks of logs, too, it was just a question of getting it to the house. She would need a wheelbarrow, and there was one in the shed. She toiled back the way she had come, this time shovelling a narrow path, fetched the wheelbarrow, and returned to the coal-house. She was a strong girl and not impatient, which was just as well, because it took time to fill the barrow and almost as long to get it to the kitchen door. She had to thump for some time before Pooley came to open it and then wait while she found coal scuttles and buckets, and then gingerly help to transfer the coal.

'My lady wants her coffee,' Pooley moaned.

'So do I,' said Jemima. 'I'm going to get a load of logs and firewood—do listen out for me, Pooley.'

The logs were easier, and lighter too. She flung them in a heap on to the kitchen floor and went back for more and then once again, this time for more coal which she left in the wheelbarrow just outside the door. She was tired now, but this afternoon she decided to get another load of wood and stack it by the barrow. The snow was holding off, but the sky was a very nasty colour and the wind, which had died down, was beginning to blow again. She stumped inside, kicked off the boots and pulled off her sodden anorak and cap, then sat down thankfully to drink the coffee Pooley had ready. She looked at the unhappy middle-aged face opposite her and decided that there was bad news. She was right.

'The telephone's out of order.'

'I'm not surprised, are you? Who did you try to get?'

'My lady wanted to speak to Martha, and then I tried the post office in the village. The line's dead.'

'Oh, well, we'll manage. I'm going to tidy myself and go and talk to Lady Manderly.'

Her employer she found sitting before the fire in the sitting-room, working at her embroidery with a martyred air. She put the canvas down with deliberation and eyed Jemima coldly.

'Ah, Jemima. Am I to have the pleasure of your company after all? I supposed I was to sit here in neglect for the whole day.'

'Perhaps Pooley didn't explain very well,' said Jemima, pleasantly matter-of-fact. 'I've been fetching and carrying coal and wood and checking the food in the house, and if I'm to cook the meals and clear the snow away from the doors, I'm afraid I can't be here as well. Pooley doesn't cook and I don't think she's strong enough to shovel snow. She's doing the housework, though.' She added kindly, 'Probably this snow won't last, but I think we ought to prepare for the worst, don't you?'

'You're being over-anxious, Jemima, but if you feel you must do these things, then by all means do them—they make a splendid excuse for leaving me to my own devices.' Lady Manderly allowed a shudder to shake her considerable frame. 'I am quite at your mercy.'

Jemima, whose feet were still cold and who saw nothing but a day of cooking and shovelling snow and humping coal before her, spoke quite sharply. 'That's nonsense, Lady Manderly. And if you're lonely, you could come down to the kitchen and help get the lunch.'

She flounced out without waiting to hear her companion's horrified answer.

Well, I'm leaving anyway, she reminded herself as she raced downstairs, and even if she sacks me I can't leave until there's a road clear.

She had another cup of coffee when she got back to the kitchen and laid a tray for Lady Manderly's lunch, set out the ingredients for an omelette, made Melba toast, and opened a can of soup. There weren't enough eggs for all of them; she and Pooley would have to be content with the soup and toast. It was a disaster that the larder should be so empty, and her opinion of Martha fell sharply. If the snow didn't thaw in a couple of days they would have to live on caviare and the other delicacies in the cupboard. She peeled potatoes—and there weren't many of those left either—cleaned some leeks and scraped the last of the carrots ready for Lady Manderly's dinner, then got back into her still damp things, pulled on the boots and went outside again. There might be potatoes in one of the outhouses, the difficulty was getting to them. She gave up presently and struggled back and forth with more logs and finding another bucket, filled that with coal before getting the shovel and starting to carve a path around the side of the house. The snow had drifted thickly against one wall and there seemed no point in trying to shift it; besides, the wind was fast becoming a gale and it was freezing. She tried the other way, working round to the front of the house, and had just cleared a narrow track when it started to snow again, gently at first but caught now and then by a gust of wind, so cold that her face was numb. She went back to the kitchen door and as she opened it remembered that the water pipes would probably freeze.

She threw off her things, got out of the boots and padded round the kitchen the pantry and several small dark empty rooms leading out of the kitchen, but she couldn't even see anything which looked like a main water tap.

And Pooley was no help, bleating about the snow, coming down in earnest now, declaring that they would all die of cold and hunger.

'Oh, stuff,' said Jemima crossly, and then seeing the look on Pooley's face, 'I'm sorry—I'm a bit tired. I'm going to see Lady Manderly . . .'

'Like that, miss?' asked her companion, appalled.

'No time to doll myself up,' said Jemima, although she might have done something about the state of her hair and face if she'd found a mirror to look into.

She hardly noticed Lady Manderly's outraged glance but plunged at once into urgent questions.

'I'm trying to find the water main tap,' she began. 'It's getting much colder and if it freezes really hard we'll get burst pipes.'

'I,' declared Lady Manderly with ice in her voice, 'am not a plumber.'

'No, I know—but could you please try and remember if there's a tap to turn off the water somewhere in this house, Lady Manderly.'

'I have no idea, Jemima, and I'm not interested in the subject. I hope I'm to have my lunch at the usual hour. You look quite unkempt. I suggest that you tidy yourself and return here; my embroidery silks are hopelessly tangled.'

Jemima, her head full of burst pipes, stared at her. 'I'm sorry, Lady Manderly, but I have to get your lunch; I'll try and find time this afternoon to see to the silks.' She made up the fire and remembered uneasily that if the weather got worse and the oil froze or the electricity went off, there would be no central heating. She was getting as bad as poor Pooley, imagining the worst.

Only by the time they had finished their lunch imagination didn't come into it; the sky had darkened and the snow, whipped into a frenzy by the wind, was piled up against the windows, so that it was already dark. They cleared the table together and went in search of lamps and candles. They found two oil lamps and a can of oil in a cupboard lining a passage leading from the kitchen to a labyrinth of small rooms, and a dozen or so candles. There was a torch too, and matches.

'Do you suppose the electricity will be on?' enquired Pooley, and shivered. 'It's ever so quiet, isn't it?'

Jemima switched on the kitchen light and said hearteningly: 'There, you see—we can switch on the television in the drawing-room, though it'll be too cold to stay there, and I'll ask Lady Manderly what the news is on the radio. I wish there was another set in the house.'

She stoked up the Aga again, prepared the vegetables for dinner, made a fruit salad from a variety of tins, and turned her attention to the chicken, while Pooley went in search of more blankets.

The wind was howling and moaning by now and although it was only mid-afternoon, it was dark. Jemima finished with the chicken and went along to see Lady Manderly and find out how she was faring. She had left her with a pile of books by the fire and a reading lamp at her elbow.

The room was in darkness save for the firelight. 'And how long must I wait for someone to turn on the lights for me?' demanded Lady Manderly.

Jemima switched on the table lamp. 'I don't think you quite understand, Lady Manderly,' she said in a voice which she strove hard to keep pleasant. 'There are only the three of us here; we've been busy all day keeping the fires going and getting meals and clearing up . . .' It didn't sound much put like that, and she was too tired to explain about fetching coal and wood—besides, she had said it all once.

She drew the heavy curtains across the windows and Lady Manderly asked grumpily: 'Is the telephone repaired yet?'

Jemima crossed the room and lifted the receiver and dialled and nothing happened. 'I am greatly inconvenienced,' declared the old lady. 'Something must be done.'

'I'll switch on the television and see if there's any news—Lady Manderly, could we have your radio on and find out what's happening?'

'If you wish. It's in my bedroom. Is there no other radio in the house?'

'We can't find one—we didn't like to look in Martha's rooms.' Jemima went to the door, longing to sit by the fire for just a little while.

She switched on the television before she went to fetch the radio, but the picture was so bad she couldn't make head or tail of it. The radio was more helpful, although hardly offering good news. Blizzards covered large parts of Scotland, gales and very low temperatures were expected; already people were stranded in cars, and villages cut off. Jemima switched off and put the set on the table at Lady Manderly's elbow without mentioning the weather conditions, then went back to the kitchen.

The Aga seemed to eat coal; she swathed herself in the cloak and opened the back door. The wheelbarrow with its load of fuel was buried under a pile of snow. She went back inside, got the coal shovel, put on gloves, and laboriously got rid of the snow, already ominously frozen, and then for want of anything better, tugged and pulled the wheelbarrow into the kitchen, where it stood untidily, the snow slowly sliding and slipping from the coal on to the floor and making great puddles.

Pooley made tea presently and Jemima carried a tray along to Lady Manderly. She poured tea for them both and sat down opposite the old lady, hopeful of making their situation clear to her, but in this she was disappointed. Lady Manderly didn't want to know, everything would be all right in the morning; she would eat her dinner earlier than usual and go to bed.

She cast an annoyed look at Jemima. 'And unless you can make yourself presentable, I will dine alone,' she pronounced.

Which was a good thing really, since it left Jemima free to get on with the cooking while Pooley crept round the house, making sure that windows and doors were secure and drawing the curtains to keep out the cold, before helping Lady Manderly to change her dress for the evening, something which Jemima found most pathetic. She herself was looking very much the worse for wear by now, but at least the chicken supreme was going to be a success; she had cooked a great pile of potatoes, arranged a salad on a side dish, and cut up the rest of the chicken for a casserole for the next day.

What with a can of soup, the potatoes puree'd, the salad and the tinned fruit, dinner was quite a success. Pooley reported that it was being eaten, as she went to and fro with the dishes and asked eagerly what they were going to eat.

'Bacon, fried potatoes, baked beans, and I've made a treacle tart—we might as well have a good supper.'

They went to bed after the nine o'clock news; it seemed to be the best place after the tale of bad weather, storms and snowdrifts and more to come. Jemima got into bed, her head still full of ways and means to get more coal into the house and how best to use the food there was, but she soon abandoned this to think about Alexander Cator. Her thoughts, though loving, were a trifle peevish too; he would be warm and well fed, probably enjoying himself with Gloria. Scotland must seem a long way off from London, as yet untroubled by snow and ice and gale force winds. She slept on the thought.

She woke at her usual time and, wrapped in her dressing gown, with a sweater over her nightie, she crept downstairs. It was still dark, but she peered from the kitchen window and was appalled to see that it was almost covered by snow and, what was far worse, the central heating wasn't working. She raked and stoked the Aga, put on the kettle and went along to the sitting-room. It was like an ice house, and the fire, long since out, merely served to make it seem colder. She cleared the ashes and left the grate empty; whether she liked it or not, Lady Manderly would have to sit in the kitchen. Pooley joined her presently, and they had a cup of tea and planned their day. 'You'd have thought that a house this size would have electric fires or gas, or something,' observed Pooley.

'Yes, but I suspect no one ever stays here during the winter and Martha and Angus have their own rooms. I do wish they hadn't locked their doors—there might be an oil stove there or calor gas . . .' They looked at each other.

'We could break down the door,' suggested Pooley, not meaning it.

'We may have to,' said Jemima, and did.

Lady Manderly didn't take kindly to the idea of sitting in her kitchen, but she was forced to agree that there was really nothing else to do about it. She came downstairs just before lunch, with Pooley trailing behind her, bearing wraps and shawls and Coco prancing behind, and she sat down in the armchair Jemima had carried through from the sitting-room. Thanks to the Aga, the room was warm and the casserole, bubbling gently, gave off a delicious smell.

Jemima, the meal on and the breakfast dishes washed, had left Pooley to tidy the bedrooms, piled on a quantity of jackets and scarves, got back into the boots and gone outside. Not without difficulty—the snow, beginning to fall again, had piled up outside the door and it was a fight to get through it. And once there, she wasn't sure where to begin. The path she had so laboriously made had disappeared again, so for that matter had the shovel and most of the shed. She found the shovel and began to clear a way to the coal; something they simply had to have at all costs. It took her the whole morning, but finally she shoved the wheelbarrow, full once more, into the kitchen.

'Coal!' enquired Lady Manderly, going purple. 'In the kitchen?'

Jemima mumbled something; it was a waste of breath trying to make the old lady understand that life was going to be a bit basic until the weather got better—or someone rescued them—Alexander, for instance. Very unlikely, she thought. His logical mind would have assessed their plight by now and decided that they would be comfortable enough in a house well stocked with food, with light and heat and plenty of hot water—only it wasn't quite like that . . .

She peeled off her wet things, got into another sweater and skirt and started on lunch.

It was almost teatime when the water gave up. Jemima had already filled everything possible with water; they could manage for days with what they had, only baths would be impossible, and she didn't dare think what would happen when the thaw set in. Lady Manderly woke from a refreshing nap and they had a cup of tea and the last of the bread, the butter spread with a miserly hand by Jemima. They had just finished when the electricity went off, came on again for a few minutes, and then went off again.

By the light of an oil lamp and a couple of candles, the kitchen looked cosy, while the supper cooked— jacket potatoes and grated cheese; Jemima fetched a pack of cards and played a fast game of Racing Demon while Pooley sat mending by the light of a candle. She was a splendid needlewoman, but Jemima doubted if the cobweb darn she was working upon would be quite up to her usual standard in such a dim light.

Their hopes that the electricity might come on again slowly faded. Jemima set the table for supper and they gathered round. It was not a very happy meal; Pooley was ill at ease and Jemima and Lady Manderly carried on the kind of conversation which the British, as a race, tend to indulge in when confronted by an awkward situation—the weather, vague world politics, the newest fashions—hardly a successful topic since both ladies had conflicting views on them—Wimbledon and the Royal Family. Not once did their talk descend to the personal, no names were mentioned and no mention was made of their return to London.

Lady Manderly rose from the table and announced:

'I shall go to bed. You're a good cook, Jemima, and the claret was exactly the one I should have chosen myself. Pooley, come with me and when I'm in bed you may fetch me a glass of hot milk and brandy.'

'There's no milk,' Jemima pointed out gently. 'Goodnight, Lady Manderly.'

Getting into bed in her icy room an hour later, she comforted herself with the thought that nothing more could happen now; they had had the worst.

She was proved to be wrong. Pooley fell downstairs and broke an arm. It was fortunate, though not from her point of view, of course, that this occurred after she had helped Lady Manderly to dress. She had been carrying the breakfast tray, which had fallen with her, scattering broken china, marmalade, a precious remnant of butter, and tea-leaves in all directions.

Jemima heard the crash and went galloping out of the kitchen, to find Pooley huddled among the debris. She knelt down beside Pooley and looked at her white face. 'Where does it hurt?'

'My arm—this one—I think it's broken, miss.'

'My poor dear! Stay still a moment, let's see if there's any other damage before we move you.'

The rest of Pooley was intact, even if sore and bruised. Jemima was about to help her on to her feet when Lady Manderly appeared at the top of the stairs. 'And what's all this?' she demanded. 'I've never heard such a noise!'

Jemima bit back a rude word or two. 'Pooley has broken her arm, Lady Manderly. Would you please go to the dining-room and get her some brandy—we've got to get her into the kitchen and see to it, but she's feeling a little faint.'

For once Lady Manderly was at a loss for words. She swept past them, scattering odds and ends all over the hall, and returned presently with the brandy.

'And now if you would give me a hand,' Jemima gave her an enquiring smile, 'I'll go on the injured side.'

Getting Pooley comfortable took some time. The break was easy enough to see; just above the wrist and not, thank heaven, an open fracture. Jemima fetched a scarf and made a sling, produced Panadol from her bag and made a pot of tea. They all sat sipping it while she wondered what was to be done. She could try to reach the village, of course. She went to the front of the house and looked out of the windows. There was nothing to be seen but snow and even if she had known the countryside well, she would never have recognised it. The sky was a frightening yellow and the wind still howled; if she started out, she was sure she wouldn't get far. She might even get lost, and then what would her two companions do?

She went back to the kitchen, refilled the cups and said cheerfully: 'They'll send a snow plough any time now, I should think. In the meantime we're warm and dry and there are still plenty of oats. I found some flour too, I'm going to make some bread. Thank heaven for the Aga!' She got up and rearranged the pillow under Pooley's injured arm. 'And you'll stay there, Pooley. I've got plenty of Panadol and you're to say the moment the pain gets bad. I'll get your tapestry work, and some books, Lady Manderly, so that you can be comfortable.'

The house had become icy. She put on another sweater while she was upstairs and took down some blankets from the beds, to tuck round her companions. 'I know none of us like the idea, but I believe it would be wise if we all slept here tonight.' She saw Lady Manderly's look of horrified outrage. 'We can't afford to be ill,' she pointed out reasonably.

The day wore on. Jemima hardly noticed it passing,

there was so much to do. She was astonished when Lady Manderly offered to wipe the supper dishes, and still more astonished when she added: 'You're a good girl, Jemima. When we've tidied up here, will you go and fetch the brandy? I think it would do us all good.' She added: 'I suppose there's no question of a bath?'

'I'm afraid not. I'll take a kettle of hot water up to your bathroom when you want it, Lady Manderly.'

Getting ready for bed was a nightmare; there was a sofa in the sitting-room which Jemima pushed into the kitchen, where it took up a frightful lot of room. But at least Lady Manderly could sleep in comparative dignity. Pooley she made comfortable in the easy chair, and for herself she carried down the duvets off the beds and curled up on the floor. She hadn't undressed Pooley, only wrapped shawls round her, but Lady Manderly had put on a nightgown and allowed herself to be tucked in, making almost no fuss.

Jemima blew out the lamp and rolled herself up in the duvets. She was so tired that she could have slept on her feet. All the same, she had a little time to think with longing of Alexander. She had managed so far, but she felt that her patience was slipping; not only that, she was just a little frightened. Anything could happen . . . if only Alexander would come! She was on the point of dozing off, but she woke herself up again; she was being silly and childish; there was no earthly reason why he should come even if he were worried about his aunt. He would only have to get in touch with the local police.

She had to get up in the night, to give Pooley more Panadol. She stayed with her until she had fallen asleep again, and was just about to blow out the candle when Lady Manderly's majestic snores ceased. 'You've been awake long, Jemima?'

'No.' whispered Jemima. 'Poor Pooley was in pain—she's had something, though, and she's asleep.'

'Come here for a minute.'

She padded over to the sofa. 'Is there anything you want?' she asked.

'No—at least, there are a great many things I should like, but it would be pointless to say so.' Lady Manderly hesitated. 'What exactly is our situation, and I don't want to be put off with untruths.'

Jemima put down her candle and perched on a chair. 'I'm not quite sure—we haven't much food left, though we can last for quite a while yet—there's plenty of oatmeal and I'm saving the other chicken. There's some flour left for another couple of loaves and tins of caviare and peaches. But we have to be careful with the water and there's no milk. Pooley ought to see a doctor soon, and unless the weather clears I can't get at the coal.'

'What do you suggest?'

'To go on as we are and keep warm. Just as soon as it's possible I'll have a go at getting to the village. Do you suppose Martha and Angus will try and get help to us?'

'Most certainly they will, but probably they're in a like case.'

'Oh, yes, I hadn't thought of that.'

'I've been thinking,' whispered Lady Manderly, 'I wonder what Gloria would have done in your place?'

'Just the same, I expect,' said Jemima untruthfully, and went back to her duvets.

They breakfasted off porridge and milkless tea and Jemima's bread, and the morning was taken up with restoring the kitchen to some sort of order, seeing to Pooley and helping Lady Manderly to dress. The cold was biting and the old lady wrapped herself in her mink coat as they left her bedroom. She looked a little pale, Jemima thought uneasily as she opened a can of soup and peeled the potatoes. She hoped it was just tiredness and lack of fresh air. When, later that morning, Lady Manderly began to sneeze and complained of a sore throat, Jemima found herself on the edge of tears. Instead, she got out the brandy bottle and made hot drinks for the three of them. She felt mean not offering Panadol to the old lady, but Pooley needed them more.

The snow stopped after midday, and she fought her way out of the door once more, only to find the snow had drifted in all directions so that she had no way of reaching the coal shed. It had frozen solid here and there, but it would be easy to step into a drift and be unable to pull herself out. She went back indoors and turned on the radio just long enough to hear the news. A voice recited an endless list of difficulties and the snow was expected to continue for the next twenty-four hours. She switched it off, more worried about Lady Manderly than the weather forecast. The old lady looked feverish and despite the fact that she was sitting bolt upright in her chair, working away at her tapestry, she looked as though she ought to have been tucked up in her bed. Jemima made the tea and went round checking her water containers. They were getting low.

'I must say,' declared Lady Manderly as they ate their supper, 'that I had no idea that a roasted potato could be so delicious, and is that a treacle tart I see on the table?'

Jemima's heart warmed to her. She had been by no means an easy employer, and no doubt once they were out of this pickle she would be as testy and selfish as she normally was, but just now she was doing her best. Poor old thing, thought Jemima, she's got a fearful cold. If only I had the water to spare I'd put her feet in a hot mustard bath.

She doled out the brandy instead; she had an idea that she had read somewhere that one shouldn't drink spirits when bitterly cold, something to do with blood pressure, but perhaps the writer had never experienced the kind of chill they were putting up with. It was worth risking anyway, because it made them all feel much better.

No one had a good night. Lady Manderly coughed and sniffed and when she did fall asleep, snored most dreadfully, Pooley was in pain and unable to sleep because of Lady Manderly, and Jemima, nipping in and out of her covers for first one and then the other, had no chance to close her eyes for more than a few minutes at a time. In the end they all dropped off as the dark night turned to a grey morning and woke late, stiff and still tired.

Porridge and tea restored them a little. Jemima helped the two ladies to make a toilet of some sort, spent a fruitless ten minutes trying to bring order to chaos in the kitchen and since it wasn't snowing, decided to have another try for the coal. There wasn't much left now and at all costs the Aga must be kept alight.

It was almost mid-morning but not really light, and the snow had hardened. Using the shovel as an awkward stick, she struggled towards where the shed would have been if she could have seen it. If the drifts around it weren't too frozen she might be able to get at the door. How she was going to get the coal back to the house was a problem she had quite overlooked.

She stood, halfway to the shed, trying to make out where it was exactly, dizzy with tiredness and the glare from the snow, wanting more than anything else to put the shovel down and curl up and go to sleep. The snow began again as she stood there, blinding her and touching off the panic she was trying to ignore. Above the wind then she thought she heard the faint beat of an engine, but it was impossible to see anything and ridiculous that she should have thought it in the first place. She turned her head away from the driving snow and tried to get her bearings; it was impossible to get lost only fifty yards or so from the house, but she wasn't sure of her direction any more. She turned again uncertainly and just for a moment the wind dropped and she saw someone coming towards her—on skis of all things!

The Professor fetched up neatly before her. 'Hullo,' he said cheerfully. Jemima stared at him as though he had been something not real at all. Feelings, strong and quite uncontrollable, surged up into her throat.

'So there you are!' she cried in a voice which would have done credit to a virago. 'Where have you been?' and burst into tears.

CHAPTER NINE

IF the Professor was surprised at this tempestuous greeting, he gave no sign, but if Jemima had been able to see clearly through her tears, she would have seen the sudden bleakness in his face. He took off his skis and the next moment she felt his arms around her. He only held her for a few seconds, while she struggled to stop crying, already regretting her words—words she had never meant to utter anyway. She had never been so glad to see anyone in her life before, but it hadn't sounded like it. She mumbled into his shoulder that she had been longing for him to come, but the wind carried away every word.

After a moment he let her go and shouted, 'We'd better go indoors before we turn into snowmen!' and turned her round. Together they made their way back to the kitchen door and he opened it and thrust her inside and followed her.

The kitchen was heavenly warm, although it looked frightfully untidy. Lady Manderly, who had been dozing, sat up straight in her chair. 'Ah, Alexander, I rather expected you would find a way of getting to us. How nice to see you!'

He bent to kiss her cheek, smiling from a tired face. When he saw Pooley sleeping off yet more Panadol, he asked: 'What happened?'

Jemima had taken off her outdoor things and padded across the kitchen floor in slippers. 'Give me those things,' she said urgently. 'I'm going to make tea in a few minutes.'

He did as she had asked and Lady Manderly asked: 'Where did you find Jemima?'

He turned and looked at her. 'Brown mouse in the snow,' he said softly, 'not quite what I expected either.' He raised his voice to answer his aunt. 'I came by helicopter and landed a few hundred yards away from the lodge. I stumbled on Jemima in the middle of nowhere.' He turned again and looked at her. 'Surely not escaping?'

'Looking for coal.' She felt shy now. Perhaps he hadn't heard her when they had met, even though he had seen her burst into shameful tears. Nothing in his manner indicated it, and she took heart from that. 'Lady Manderly's got a very bad cold and Pooley's broken her arm,' she volunteered, and blushed because she was telling him someting he could quite well see for himself. But he only nodded at her gently. He hadn't missed the blush, but he didn't comment on it. 'We'd better splint that arm,' was his only comment, and when Jemima gave him a questioning look: 'I'm a doctor as well as an endocrinologist, you know. Now let's see; what can we use for splints?'

He stood in the middle of the room dominating it, and Jemima at least was sure that all their worries were at an end. He looked surprisingly elegant; she admired him silently as she laid his things by the Aga to dry.

'Still going to Huntsman for your suits, I see,' commented Lady Manderly in a sodden voice, and sneezed.

'Of course, Aunt.' He was rolling up his shirt sleeves, having taken off his jacket.

'And your shirts?' She sneezed again.

'I prefer Turnbull and Asser.'

How can they talk about shirts when we're in need of a good meal and a wash? thought Jemima, and made the tea.

By the time she had poured it, the Professor had rooted round the mess in the kitchen and come up with an empty drawer which he proceeded to take apart and fashion into two splints with the potato knife. Pooley had woken up by now and he was talking to her in a reassuring way while he cut one of the kitchen curtains into strips. Jemima, watching him, felt ashamed that she hadn't thought of doing that herself.

'Tea?' he asked, looking up suddenly and catching her gazing at him. He smiled to melt her very bones. 'I'm hungry, or are we out of food?'

She produced the last of the bread and sliced it and used up the remains of the butter—a reckless thing to do, but she felt that it was an occasion.

She sipped her tea, only half listening to his quiet talk with Lady Manderly. Coco had climbed on to his knee and he was stroking the woolly grey head. Jemima longed to ask just how he had got to them, but he might fob her off with one of his nasty smiles. She held her tongue, happily unaware of her appearance, which was regrettably tatty and grimy, but even if she had given it a thought she wouldn't have cared, though, she was tired and suddenly dispirited. None of this was real, and when they got back to London, he would look at her in that mocking way he had. They lived in two different worlds, he and she, and it would be as well if she remembered that.

His voice disturbed her thoughts. 'Come over here, Jemima, and steady this arm, will you?'

He was very gentle, but Pooley fainted from fright before he had touched her.

'Good. Hold her arm above the elbow and when I say pull, pull.'

It took only a moment to straighten the bones; by the time he was binding on the splints, Pooley was recovering.

'All done, my dear,' he assured her calmly. 'Jemima will give you some brandy.'

'This is all there is,' Jemima said apologetically. 'We've all been drinking it.'

He smiled slowly. 'A very good idea too. Jemima, go and pack Pooley's things, and I'll take her to Fort William; they're cut off there, but there's enough of everything to keep them going for days and the hospital's got emergency generators.' And when Pooley murmured protestingly. 'Don't worry, as soon as this weather clears, we'll have you back in London. And you won't be alone. Lady Manderly and Jemima will be there too.'

'What do you plan for us?' asked his aunt.

'Why, a day or two there, Aunt and then Belling can

come up by train and see you all safely back home. I'll
have to go back as soon as possible, otherwise I'd stay
with you.'

Jemima had wrapped herself in one of the shawls
and started for the door. She had reached it when the
Professor caught up with her. 'I'll help you,' he
offered. 'You'll have to pack for everyone.'

It was too cold to talk in the hall or on the stairs,
and Pooley's room was no better.

'The cases are in the boxroom at the end of the passage,' she told him, and when he returned with the
first of them: 'Are we all going together?'

'Lord no! Pooley first, I'll drop her off at the hospital; there's bound to be a taxi at the airfield. I'll come
back for aunt and her luggage and settle her in at a
hotel, and then come back for you. You won't mind
being alone here for a little while?'

Jemima wondered what he would do if she said yes.
'Not in the least,' she told him coolly.

He went back for the rest of the luggage, and she
started to pack Pooley's things. Thank heaven they had
none of them brought much with them. She was
shivering by the time she had finished. The Professor
took the case downstairs and she went along to Lady
Manderly's room. He came back again before she had
done more than open the first drawer.

She looked at him over her shoulder. 'There's no
need for you to stay here,' she pointed out. 'I'll call
you when I'm ready. It's far too cold.'

He took no notice of this but came into the room
and sat down on the end of the bed. 'Why were you so
furious when you saw me?' he wanted to know.

Jemima paused in her packing. 'I—I was surprised.'

'And yet I had the strong impression that you were
expecting me . . .' His voice was silky.

Jemima, folding tentlike nighties, didn't look at him. 'What rubbish!' she said crossly. 'Why on earth should I expect you of all people?'

'Why indeed? I was hoping you could—or would— tell me.'

'Well, I can't. How are you going to get Pooley to the helicopter?'

'Now that's a question I'm still pondering. But whatever we decide it must be soon. It's roughly fifty miles—no, less by air, say half an hour, taking into account loading and offloading and so forth—I'll return for my aunt and then come back for you. By then it will be growing dark. You're not afraid? It may be a little awkward.'

'Not in the least,' declared Jemima robustly, her insides quite jellied at the idea. 'It will be nice to have a hot bath and a proper meal.' She started on a pile of woollies. 'I do hope Lady Manderly will be all right, she's got a shocking cold. She's been wonderful, you know.'

The Professor said thoughtfully: 'No one has ever called her that before!' He got off the bed. 'May I have one of those scarves?' and when she handed it to him: 'I'm going to take the first of the luggage to the helicopter; I'll be back for Pooley in a short time.' He lounged over to the window. 'It's not snowing at the moment, I'd best be on my way.'

He wandered back to her, bent and kissed her hard and swiftly and went away.

Jemima finished packing Lady Manderly's things, not allowing herself to think about him at all, and went back downstairs to the kitchen presently.

Lady Manderly was sitting exactly as she had left her, but Pooley had got to her feet and was peering fearfully out of the window. She looked round as

Jemima went in. 'I'll never be able to get there,' she moaned unhappily. 'All that snow, I'm sure to fall over . . . I don't want to go . . .'

'You'll do as the Professor tells you,' observed Lady Manderly hoarsely.

'You'll be perfectly safe,' Jemima told her bracingly. 'The Professor wouldn't attempt it if he wasn't quite sure he'd succeed.' She had joined Pooley at the window. 'Look, here he is coming back; it can't be far, and the snow's very hard.' She started wrapping Pooley's coat round her and buttoning it. 'You've got one good arm,' she pointed out, 'and think how lovely it will be to sleep in a bed tonight and have someone to look after you.'

'You've been doing that,' said Pooley. 'I don't know what we'd have done without you, miss.'

Professor Cator's cheerful voice interrupted her. 'Ready?' he enquired, and waited patiently while Jemima wound a scarf round Pooley's head and tied it firmly. There was only one pair of wellingtons, and, she had thrust Pooley's reluctant feet into them. 'And for heaven's sake bring them back with you,' she begged the Professor, 'so we can use them later.'

She watched them go, the Professor once more on his skis, an arm round Pooley's waist, hauling her along beside him. When they had gone round a great drift by the garage, she turned away from the window.

'What about lunch?' asked Lady Manderly.

Jemima stopped dead in her tracks. 'Lunch—oh, my goodness, the poor man's had nothing to eat—only that tea and bread and butter, and he looked so tired.'

'He'll snatch a sandwich before he comes back for me,' said her companion comfortably. 'He's always been able to look after himself. What is there left to eat, Jemima?'

Jemima went to the cupboard and surveyed its contents. 'Caviare, a tin of pâté and the oatmeal. Shall it be porridge?'

'Since there's nothing else, but you may open the caviare, Jemima, I'll have that first. You don't suppose there are any biscuits?'

'No, Lady Manderly, but we can have a cup of tea.'

She set about cooking the porridge and boiling the kettle, and presently they ate their meal while Lady Manderly discoursed in a gruff voice on the delights of caviare, when and where she had eaten it and in whose company. Jemima listened with half an ear and an eye on the clock, her thoughts almost entirely of Alexander.

'You're not listening,' declared Lady Manderly. 'You needn't worry about Alexander. He is, as I've already said, perfectly capable of looking after himself.' Jemima didn't answer and her companion went on: 'You're not a pretty girl, but given the right clothes and a good hairdresser you would do well enough; you have a certain air about you. It's time that Alexander settled down.'

Her cold was making her feverish, thought Jemima The quicker she was got into a warm bed and properly fed, the better. She cleared away the dishes and left the kettle singing on the Aga. Alexander would want tea when he got back. And I must stop thinking of him as Alexander, she told herself sharply.

He arrived almost silently, his coming muffled by the sound of the wind. Jemima caught sight of him coming round the garage and opened the door.

'My God, it's cold,' he said. 'Any tea?' He smiled at her. 'Will you help my aunt to get into her things? I'll have that tea and then get the rest of her cases on board and come back for her. Pooley's safe and sound in hospital; they're going to set that arm and put it into plaster, and she'll be able to join you at the hotel some time tomorrow.'

He swallowed the tea and went upstairs for the cases and Jemima urged Lady Manderly into a variety of woollies, her mink coat, and the boots, tied a scarf securely round her head and sat her down to drink some of the tea while the Professor, the cases tied on to his back and Coco under one arm, set off once more.

He was back very shortly. 'I'll be as quick as I can,' he told Jemima. 'Pack the rest of your things and then come down here and stay by the stove.' He glanced at the clock. 'Don't put any more coal on to it, and rake it out as well as you can when it gets low.' His eyes searched her quiet face. 'What a splendid girl you are!' This time he didn't kiss her. She watched him toiling through the snow, his aunt, her not inconsiderable weight supported by his arm, contriving to look regal even in wellington boots.

She went upstairs presently and finished packing her own things, then brought the case down to the kitchen. The house was quiet so that the wind sounded more eerily than before. Lady Manderly had taken her radio with her and there was nothing to break the silence. Jemima poked up the Aga and made more tea and watched the clock's hands creep at a snail's pace round its face. She lighted the lamp soon; it wasn't dark, but it seemed more cheerful, and presently she lighted the candles too, rather recklessly. Suppose Alexander couldn't get back? He had told her to let the stove out and the kitchen was already getting chilly. She got up and walked around, stopping to look out of the window—a silly thing to do, because she knew quite well that there was no chance of his return for another hour at least. Lady Manderly would demand his full attention until she was settled in at the hotel, and that might be miles away from the airstrip.

She found an old cookery book presently and sat down at the table close to the lamp and passed the time choosing various menus. 'French onion soup,' she said aloud, 'and then grilled sole and boeuf en croûte and a soufflé harlequin with lashings of cream.' She gave a great sigh. 'If only someone would ask me out to dinner that's what I'd choose.'

She got up and began to walk about again. The Aga was very low now and the room was cold. She put on another sweater and looked at the clock. Alexander should have arrived by now. A pang of pure panic shot through her; he'd run out of fuel, he'd had an accident, he was dead . . .

He opened the door and walked in, and only by a superhuman effort did Jemima manage not to burst into tears.

'Ready?' he asked, just as though he'd been gone for a couple of minutes instead of the best part of two hours, and when she nodded, went over to the Aga, raked it out, blew out the candles and the lamp and picked up her case. 'Let's go, then.'

He sounded so abrupt and impatient that she didn't speak, only followed him wordlessly outside. He must be very tired by now, she knew, and the least she could do was not to waste a second of his time. He tied the case on his back and caught her by the arm, slipped on his skis, and set off. It wasn't as difficult as she had expected. The boots were too big, of course and she floundered a bit, determined to keep up with him. Once or twice she went into deep snow and he hauled her out, the snow melting down her cold legs inside the boots, so that her feet became numb. She began to think that they had lost the helicopter, and then suddenly there it was, only yards away.

Even if she hadn't loved him she would have admired him for ever for the neat speed in which he got her case, the skis and themselves on board. The helicopter seemed very small; she hoped nervously that it would stay up in the air as they rose from the ground and she closed her eyes.

'Perfectly safe,' said the Professor's calm voice. 'I've been flying for some years.' The faint mockery in his voice made her open her eyes at once.

'I'm not in the least nervous,' she assured him coldly, and then as he swung round in a half circle, shut them again.

It was very nearly dark by now, but the snow threw an uncanny light over the countryside. Jemima took a look from time to time and decided that she didn't much like it; she had never been so thankful to see the airport's lights.

It was like being a child again. She was lifted out of the helicopter, told to do this, that and the other thing and obeyed without question. The whole process was vague until she found herself in the foyer of the hotel with the Professor beside her.

He took her arm and went over to the reception desk where he was given a key which he put into her hand. 'Go up to your room and—er—tidy yourself. We'll have dinner in half an hour. And don't go to sleep!'

'What about Lady Manderly? I must . . .'

'I'll go and see her now. You shall go and say good night to her after we've had dinner. She will have hers in her room.'

Jemima was too weary to argue—besides, she was well aware that it would be of no use. She followed the bellboy into the lift without another word.

Her room was warm and comfortable and the bed was inviting. She tore her eyes from it and undressed, had a shower and took her things out of her case, regretting that she had nothing spectacular to wear. Another skirt and a blouse with a thin sweater over it was the best she could manage. Her hair needed a wash, but there wasn't time. With a couple of minutes in hand she made her way down to the foyer.

The Professor was waiting for her. He took her into the bar and sat her down. 'What we both need is a drink,' he said pleasantly, 'and then a meal.' He smiled at her. 'How nice you look,' he observed. 'Although I must say you looked pretty good this morning.'

She blushed, because of course he was teasing her, and accepted the sherry he offered her. 'I won't ask if you'd like brandy,' he went on. 'All three of you must have drunk deep of that!'

He was teasing. She smiled and sipped her sherry, feeling lightheaded. She was going to have dinner with him, for the first—and almost for certain the last time too. The prospect rendered her silent, so that her share of the conversation was an occasional yes or no.

But over dinner she found her tongue again. She was going to enjoy her evening, since she wasn't likely to have another one like it. When he asked her what she would like to eat she said instantly: 'Oh, French onion soup, grilled sole and boeuf en croûte,' and then seeing his amused look: 'Oh no, I'm sorry, that's what I chose while I was waiting for you. There was an old cookery book and I picked out what I would most like . . . it was just something to do.'

'A sound choice.' He beckoned the waiter and held a low-voiced conversation with him. When the man had gone he said: 'They can't manage the beef, it would take too long, but I'm told the spare ribs are excellent.

Will you try those instead?'

'Oh, I didn't mean . . . there was no need to go to all that trouble . . . it was only . . .'

'My dear girl, after the days you've just been through, if you'd asked for the moon, I would have done my best to get it for you.' He sat back in his chair, looking at her. 'Such a small mouse of a girl facing up to a situation which would have daunted anyone twice your size. I can imagine my aunt was hardly the easiest of companions, and Pooley may be splendid with the mending and ironing, but I don't fancy she could stand up to an emergency.' He broke off as they were served their soup. 'Thank God for food,' he commented.

'When did you last have a meal?' asked Jemima, all her motherly instincts aroused.

'Breakfast—very early this morning.'

'What happened to . . .' She broke off and bit her lip. 'Of course, you were at the lodge by then, and I didn't give you anything to eat. I'm truly sorry. I could have made you a bowl of porridge . . .'

'I never eat porridge.' He sounded aloof, but the sherry on her empty insides had made her slightly reckless. She waited until their plates had been removed and replaced by the sole. 'Did Gloria mind you coming?' she asked, and sipped the white wine in her glass.

'I hardly had time to tell her,' he told her carelessly. 'Have you received the replies to your advertisement?' he added, 'I got my secretary to see to it.'

She had gone a little pale at the snub, but it had been her own fault after all. 'Yes, thank you,' she tried to match her voice with his. 'There were three of them.'

'Any good?'

She busied herself with the sole so that she wouldn't have to look at him. 'Oh, yes, they're all three rather nice, I think, I'm not sure which to choose. I've written to them all and I'll see which I like the best.'

'In London?'

Jemima thought rapidly; if she said no he might smell a rat. 'One is—one is somewhere in Hampstead, of the others, the one I like best is somewhere in the Midlands. I can never quite remember the places there.'

The Professor was watching her intently. He said coolly: 'It might be a pleasant change for you. My aunt will, of course, give you a splendid reference.'

'How kind,' said Jemima forlornly.

Her glass was whisked away and she was given red wine with the beef. She sipped it appreciatively. 'Claret?' she essayed.

'Indeed yes. Will your duties be the same as those at my aunt's house?'

'I think very similar.'

'Another old lady?'

She frowned down at her plate. How persistent he was!

'An elderly couple living in an annexe of their daughter's house.' She started to improvise. 'I shall drive the car for them and that sort of thing.'

The Professor hid a smile. 'It only remains for me to wish you every success. Although I can't think why I should have made such a mistake—I was under the impression that you were going to train for something . . .'

Jemima choked over a morsel of potato. 'Oh, but I am going to, but—but one has to put one's name down some months ahead.' She hunted feverishly for some career she might follow and could think of none on the spur of the moment, and the Professor, watching her telltale face, took pity on her.

'Of course, I hadn't thought of that. Now what would you like for dessert?'

'An ice cream with chocolate sauce and nuts, please.'

He ordered it gravely, chose the cheese board for himself and began to talk about nothing in particular. They had their coffee at the table and presently he suggested that she might like to go to bed. 'I'll be leaving in the morning—will you have breakfast with me? Is eight o'clock too early for you?'

'No—no, not a bit. Must you go in the morning?'

'Yes, I have some afternoon appointments and an evening engagement.' With Gloria, thought Jemima, then thanked him nicely for the dinner and wished him goodnight.

She went to Lady Manderly's room first. That lady, having dined well, was sitting in her bed reading. She put down her book as Jemima knocked and observed: 'There you are. I hope Alexander looked after you?'

'Yes, thank you, Lady Manderly. Can I do anything for you?'

'No, I think not. I shall stay in bed tomorrow and throw off this cold. You'll have to go to the hospital and see how Pooley is and arrange for her to come here as soon as possible.' She nodded dismissal. 'Come and see me at nine o'clock tomorrow morning, Jemima.'

Jemima went to her room. She was very sleepy, but she made herself wash her hair and then lay in the bath, dreaming. Such a waste of time, she told herself crossly, falling into bed and almost instantly asleep.

At least her hair was clean, she decided, looking at her still tired face in the morning. She slapped on some make-up, brushed her hair until it gleamed, took a look out of the window at the dark morning outside, and went down to the dining-room.

The Professor was already there. His good morning was cheerfully impersonal, as were his queries as to whether she had slept well and how she felt. She had barely reached the toast and marmalade of a substantial meal when he excused himself. 'I didn't go and see my aunt last night,' he explained. 'I must say goodbye to her now.'

Somehow it wasn't what she had expected. After a moment she said: 'Oh, yes, of course. Well, goodbye, Professor Cator, and thank you for all you've done. It must have been most inconvenient.'

He didn't answer that, but said carelessly: 'I'll see you when you get back.'

She watched him go; she wouldn't see him again, she would take care to be gone before then. She went on with her breakfast feeling utterly miserable, wondering what he and his aunt would have to say to each other.

She would have been surprised.

'We shall see you in London, Alexander.' Lady Manderly a majestic figure in bed despite her cold and a red nose. 'I'm not sure what Jemima intends to do— she has several jobs lined up, I believe.'

'She told you that too?' He was leaning over the end of the bed, smiling a little. 'It's a nuisance, but I have to be away for several days, but I doubt if she'll leave you immediately. In any case . . .' He talked for a few minutes and his aunt nodded in agreement.

'You intend to marry her?'

He was still smiling. 'Oh, yes. I find I can't contemplate life without her.'

'Does she know this?'

'No—I've taken great care . . . She doesn't approve of me entirely, you see, and she might run away before I can change her mind for her.' He went round the bed and kissed her cheek. 'Goodbye, aunt. I shall send Belling up just as soon as the trains are running again. That shouldn't be long now.'

Jemima spent a busy morning, which was just as well because she had little time to think about her own problems. Pooley had to be visited, and since the doctor saw no reason why she shouldn't join Lady Manderly at the hotel, Jemima called a taxi, took her back, engaged a room and went along with her to see Lady Manderly. She left the two ladies together, thoughtfully ordered coffee for them, and went out into the town to buy the things her employer required.

She liked the town. Its main street bustled with life despite the shocking weather. She worked through her list, had coffee in a pleasant small café, and went back to the hotel, to find Pooley happy once more, re-packing Lady Manderly's cases, tut-tutting over the way the things had been folded, and making plans for borrowing an iron so that everything could be pressed.

'So fortunate that it's my left arm in plaster,' she confided to Jemima as they had lunch together. 'It hardly bothers me at all. My lady says you're leaving us, miss? When's that?'

'I'm not sure,' said Jemima cautiously. 'I haven't got a job yet, but I've three interviews lined up for when we get back. If you're going to be busy this afternoon, I'll take Coco for a walk and then go and sit with Lady Manderly. We can play cards or something.'

The day passed, and the next. Lady Manderly, cossetted in bed, recovered rapidly. 'I trust Belling will come shortly,' she observed to Jemima over tea in her room. 'I'm fit to travel and I'm told the trains are running again. Alexander saw no reason why we shouldn't go back to London at the first opportunity.' She cast a sharp eye upon Jemima. 'He telephones me each evening.'

'Then I expect Belling will be here tomorrow, Lady Manderly.' Jemima spoke calmly, but she couldn't stop the colour creeping into her cheeks at the mention of the Professor's name.

Belling arrived that evening quite late. Lady Manderly had already gone to bed, but Jemima was in the hotel lounge reading and he came straight to her. 'Nice to see you, miss,' he greeted her. 'I've everything arranged for tomorrow morning, if that can be managed. I believe Professor Cator telephoned Lady Manderly earlier this evening, so she'll have had warning. You'll be in London before tomorrow night.'

'How nice to see you too, Belling, and to have everything arranged. Have you a room? Shall I get one for you, and what about something to eat?'

'A room's been booked for me, miss, and I had a meal before I came here.'

'Then I think I'd better go to bed and pack my things. What time do we leave?'

'Ten o'clock, miss.' He smiled at her. 'I've arranged for a taxi to take us to the station, if you could manage to get my lady ready to leave.'

'I will. I'll pop along and see Pooley now. Goodnight, Belling.'

The return to London went without a hitch. Jemima had been expecting delays, even a train missed because Lady Manderly couldn't be hurried, but the old lady proved herself quite amenable to being got up at an early hour and conveyed, with Belling, Pooley, and Jemima to sustain her, to the station. Jemima, subsiding into a corner of the compartment which had been booked for Lady Manderly's sole use, settled Coco on her knee and heaved a sigh of relief. Her companion's cold was still severe and since she dropped off to sleep very shortly after they left Fort William, Jemima had nothing to do but stare out of the window at the snow outside. But not for long-presently Belling, with a steward at his heels, came with coffee, and later they all went along to the dining car, where Pooley and Belling discreetly disappeared again, and Jemima, with Coco still in tow, shared a table with Lady Manderly, who, at her most amiable, kept up a steady flow of small talk. She dozed again during the afternoon, though, and woke refreshed, when tea was brought with Pooley and Belling trailing it to make sure that they had everything they required. Never had Jemima travelled four hundred and ninety-seven miles in such comfort, nor with such a heavy heart.

Lady Manderly's car, with her usual chauffeur, met them at the station and they were driven away without delay, with Coco sitting on Jemima's knee. Belling and Pooley had taken the luggage and were borne away in a taxi.

Lady Manderly was silent now and Jemima contented herself with looking out of the window and seeing the business of the lighted streets. She wasn't very sure of her whereabouts, and presently she frowned in puzzlement. They had reached the West End by now, but as far as she could see they weren't going to Lady Manderly's house. The car had turned away from its direction and was going north through Portland Place, to turn off into New Cavendish Street and thence into Welbeck Street and then to turn once more into a small quiet street lined with Georgian houses. Here they stopped and Lady Manderly said in satisfied tones: 'Ah, we are here. Get out, Jemima, and tell Lucas to come back for us in two hours' time.'

Mystified, Jemima did as she was told and then, obedient to Lady Manderly's command, beat a genteel tattoo on the brass door knocker. Like many houses of that type, this one was tall and thin and rather secret, with discreetly curtained bay windows and a black-painted door with a fanlight over it.

The door was opened almost at once by a very tall, very thin elderly man, who bowed slightly, greeted them with dignity and ushered them into a narrow hall, discreetly lighted, panelled in white-painted wood, and from which several doors led. They were barely inside when one of these doors opened and Professor Cator came out.

'Ah, Aunt—so you're safely back in London. Mrs Clegg shall take you upstairs. Dinner will be in half an hour; we shall have ample time to have a drink beforehand. You know where the drawing-room is.' He had kissed her lightly on the cheek, now he smiled briefly at Jemima as an elderly woman came through a door at the end of the hall.

'Good evening, my lady,' she said pleasantly, and added with a smile: 'And you, miss,' and without further ado led the way up the curving staircase, to show Lady Manderly into a bedroom and then open the door next to it and wave Jemima inside. 'The draw-ing-room is on the right of the stairs, miss,' she advised, and went away.

Jemima sat down on the edge of the bed and took stock of the room. It gave her a chance to settle her pulse rate too; it had shot up at the sight of the Professor and her insides were gyrating. She forced herself to stop thinking of him and concentrated on her surroundings. They were charming—applewood and yew, chintz and a carpet to lose one's feet in. After a minute or two she got up and opened doors. A bathroom, so perfect it would be a pity to spoil its pristine freshness by taking a bath; a huge clothes cupboard, and another smaller one in which to put one's luggage, presumably. She washed her face and hands and did her hair, then sat down and did her face very carefully. It didn't make much difference, she decided, but at least she felt better.

She was undecided about whether to knock on Lady Manderly's door when she was ready, but the sound of that lady's voice from somewhere below sent her downstairs. Mrs Clegg had said the door on the right; she opened it and went inside.

Lady Manderly was enthroned in a wing back chair by a cheerful fire and her nephew was sitting on the arm of a chair opposite her. He got up as Jemima put her head round the door and crossed the room to take the door handle from her and shut it. 'Come and sit down,' he advised. 'Will you have sherry or something else?'

Jemima sat. 'Sherry, please,' she answered in a calm little voice, and once more took stock of her surroundings. The Professor lived in style, she saw that at once—lovely old furniture, a beautiful room with a high ceiling and pale walls hung with paintings. She accepted her glass and when he asked her politely if she had quite recovered from the stay at the lodge, answered him with equal politeness, while her ears were stretched for the sound of Gloria's voice. She would surely join them. The Professor was wearing a black tie, so he would be going out later, presumably with the girl. But there was no sign of her and she wasn't mentioned.

Presently they went across the hall to a smaller room,

panelled in yew wood, with a table and chairs to match and elaborate velvet curtains at the window, and here the tall thin man, addressed as Clegg, served their dinner: lobster patties, served hot, sole Véronique, and boeuf en croûte. Jemima blushed when she saw it and avoided the Professor's eye, although she was perfectly aware that he was looking at her. Mrs Clegg's own rich custard tart finished the meal before they went back to the drawing-room for their coffee. And all the time the conversation had been airy nothings, with an occasional side tracking on Lady Manderly's part while she expounded an opinion at length.

They didn't sit long over their coffee. Lady Manderly put down her cup and said: 'We must be going, Alexander, and you will be wanting to go to this reception. You may telephone me in the morning before you leave.'

He accompanied them to the street door, bade his aunt goodnight and then at the last minute, bent and kissed Jemima's cheek. She stared up at him, not knowing what to say and in the end saying nothing at all. She would have choked over 'Goodbye'.

It was well after nine o'clock by now. She saw Lady Manderly into her house, collected her case and started to walk down to the shop. She had written to Shirley asking her to expect them one day soon, although she wasn't sure when, and now all she longed for was her small room and her bed.

Lady Manderly had bidden her goodnight without saying more, only to remind her to be prompt on the following morning. It seemed a bit of an anticlimax after the excitements of the last few days, but it served to get her feet back on to firm ground once again. Tomorrow she would tell Lady Manderly she was leaving; she had already said so, and the old lady had understood quite clearly that Jemima was free to go once they returned to London.

She saw the shop was closed, of course, but the lights were on in the flat above. Jemima rang the bell and Shirley came to let her in.

'Hello, ducks,' she said warmly, 'nice to see yer again. Yer room's ready. Want a bite ter eat? Mum's still up.'

'Oh, Shirley, it's lovely to see you. No, I've had my supper, are you and Mrs Adams all right? It seems ages . . .'

Shirley looked her over with a critical eye, standing in the middle of the shop floor. 'I can't say 'as 'ow yer look any better for the change.' She picked up Jemima's case and started upstairs. ''ad a rough time in Scotland, did yer?'

'Well, yes, it was rather awful.' Jemima's voice made Shirley turn and look at her.

'Tell us about it tomorrow, eh?'

'Yes, I will. I've got to be at work by nine o'clock.'

They said goodnight, and Mrs Adams poked her head round the kitchen door and called goodnight too.

The room was poky and unlived-in, even with the little gas fire burning it seemed cold. Jemima unpacked and went to bed and cried herself to sleep.

There was no chance to mention leaving to Lady Manderly until the afternoon. Jemima was kept busy answering letters and the telephone, writing cheques and accepting the invitations waiting for Lady Manderly, and when those were done, Coco had to be taken for her walk. They lunched together, but since Jemima had a notebook and pen by her plate and Lady Manderly rattled off directions like bullets from a gun, it was hardly a sociable meal.

'I shall take a nap,' declared the old lady. 'Take Coco

out, Jemima, and be back at three o'clock.' She sailed
from the room, but Jemima caught her up in the hall.

'Lady Manderly, we agreed that I might leave as
soon as we returned here. I should like to go tomorrow
if I may.'

Lady Manderly's cheeks went mauve. 'Impossible!
How am I to manage? I never heard such nonsense!'

'All the same, that's what we agreed. I said I would
go to Scotland with you provided I might leave when
we returned here. I told you that I had several jobs to
choose from . . .'

Lady Manderly stood glowering at her. Alexander,
bother the man, was in Vienna, of all places, for the
next four days. She conjured up a smile. 'Yes, of
course, you're quite right, Jemima. Will you oblige me
by staying for the remainder of this week?' And when
she saw the stubborn look on Jemima's face: 'Until the
day after tomorrow?' After all, Alexander might be able
to fly back a day or two earlier.

Jemima hesitated. 'Very well, Lady Manderly, until
the day after tomorrow.'

'And where will you go?' enquired Lady Manderly
cunningly. Alexander would never forgive her if she
didn't find out.

'Oxford,' said Jemima instantly, because that was the
place which came most readily to her mind. 'My
friends there are driving me up to an interview in the
Midlands.'

She hoped it sounded genuine—after all, she had
mentioned a job in the Midlands. Lady Manderly
seemed to think so, for she nodded briskly. 'Well, take
Coco out now and we'll get on with the letters when
you return.'

It was a busy afternoon. Jemima left at six o'clock,
feeling tired and aimless. She would have liked to have

gone straight to her room, but Mrs Adams and Shirley were waiting for her and she spent the evening regaling them with the story of her adventures in Scotland.

She spent the next evening scanning the vacancies columns in the papers, but there was nothing at all. She paid her rent, explained that she had given up working for Lady Manderly, and told Mrs Adams that she would soon get another job and in the meantime could she stay on with her. It was Shirley who came to her room that evening and suggested that she might like to fill in a couple of weeks serving in the shop. 'Mum wants ter see 'er sister at Southend—I'll look after the post office, but I'll need help. Mum says you can 'ave yer room rent-free and yer food if you'll do it.'

'It'll give me a chance to pick and choose a new job,' said Jemima hopefully. 'Yes, Shirley, I'll be glad to.'

She bade Lady Manderly goodbye the next day, feeling mean. If it hadn't been for Alexander she would have stayed with her, but the sooner she cut him right out of her life the better, and this resolve was strengthened that afternoon as she took Coco for their last walk together. They were nearing the house when a car drew up alongside and Gloria's voice hailed her.

'Hullo, Jemima—still toiling away, I see. You should be like me and get yourself a man.' She smiled with malice. 'Though there's only one man you fancy, isn't there? Don't worry, I'm not jealous, I daresay he's brightened your dull life for a few weeks. It's better to have loved and lost, etc,' she laughed a gay little trill, and drove on, leaving Jemima shaking.

Belling and Pooley and Cook seemed sorry to see her go, but Lady Manderly didn't seem to mind in the least. Her goodbye was casual in the extreme.

Mrs Adams left the next morning and Jemima went

to work in the shop. She quickly discovered that she didn't like it over-much; there was a lot of standing about and she wasn't quick enough handing out the right papers to the regular customers, but at least she had a bed and food, and a small hoard of money. She wrote cheerfully to Dick, being vague about a new job, and whenever she had a moment to spare, studied the vacancies. Of Lady Manderly there was no sign, of course. Although she lived close by, it was another world, markedly different from the one Jemima now lived in. She had given Lady Manderly the address of her friends in Oxford so that letters could be forwarded there, and written off to them to explain, although there was really no need. There was no one to write to her; her friends had gradually ceased to correspond and Dick always sent his letters to the shop.

The week went slowly by, the days long and tiring, for as well as the shop there were meals to get and the flat to keep tidy. Of course Shirley helped, but she had her boy-friend most evenings and if they went out, and they mostly did, Jemima filled her evenings with housework. It stopped her from thinking.

They had decorated the shop with tinsel and paper chains, which somehow made it shabbier than ever, and the light had to be on almost all day now. The second week brought cold dark weather with it, and Jemima longed for Saturday to come. Mrs Adams would be back and, job or no job, she would take herself off for a few days—indeed, she would have to, as she learned that evening that Mrs Adams and Shirley were to spend Christmas with the boy-friend's family.

On the Saturday she went down to the shop earlier than usual. Shirley had to go to the dentist and had closed the post office, leaving Jemima in charge. A steady stream of men on their way to work tramped in and out, their wet shoes leaving muddy marks all over the floor. Jemima put out more papers, and began to tidy the magazines. When the doorbell rang and the door was flung open she turned round sharply; the door wasn't all that strong on its hinges. Her mouth was open to say so, but not a word came out, although it stayed open in surprise.

Alexander stood there, quite out of place in his beautifully tailored topcoat. He said through his teeth. 'Well, I'm damned! I've torn Oxford apart looking for you.'

'Why?' asked Jemima baldly.

'Because that's where you're supposed to be. Only by the merest chance did Belling remember that one of the maids thought she'd seen you here. I've been a fool, I should have come here straight away.' He frowned at her. 'I didn't know you were lying,' he added evenly.

She had nothing to say to this, but when the silence had gone on too long she asked in a small voice: 'Did you want a paper?'

'No,' said Alexander. 'I want you, Jemima. My brown mouse, my darling brown mouse of a girl.'

She looked at him with troubled eyes, although her heart sang. 'But you can't—you've got Gloria.'

He shook his head. 'What makes you think that because I took her around I wanted to marry her? I don't care two straws for the girl, never did. She was useful camouflage while I was doing my best to get you interested in me.'

'You didn't!' squeaked Jemima indignantly. 'You laughed at me, and when you weren't doing that you ignored me.'

'If I hadn't done that I should have eaten you with a spoon.'

She laughed at that, and then shook her head. 'But I saw Gloria last week; she said . . .' She blushed as she remembered, and the Professor laughed suddenly and came round the counter.

'Shall I guess?' he asked softly. 'Do you love me just a little, my dearest girl? I shall probably be a bad husband, but I shall love you all my life—indeed, I can think of nothing on this earth that I want to do more.'

He pushed aside a pile of *Daily Mirrors* and caught her close and kissed her; and when she started to say something, he kissed her again, even harder.

'I'm taking you back to Aunt's house, you can stay with her until we get married.'

'Oh, but I can't stay there, Lady Manderly wouldn't like it.'

'Yes, she will, she fancies you as a niece.' He kissed her again. 'And I fancy you as a wife, my darling.'

The doorbell went again and a large untidy man ambled in. 'I'll have the *Sun*.' He looked without much interest upon the Professor, standing with Jemima locked in his arms.

'Help yourself to anything you fancy, my dear chap,' said the Professor largely.

When he had gone, Jemima said severely: 'That won't do at all, you know: he could have cleared the shop.'

'How soon can we close this infernal place?'

'Not until Shirley comes back from the dentist, and then I must explain and pack my things and . . .'

'Let us take one thing at a time,' declared Alexander. 'We can sit here and get to know each other, for a start.'

'How?'

'Like this, my darling.' And he bent to kiss her again.

A WORD ABOUT THE AUTHOR

Betty Neels sandwiched the time for writing her first novel between the hours she spent on various household chores. Her husband and daughter fondly referred to her scribbles, in school exercise books, as "mother's little hobby."

Betty's husband, Johannes, is a Dutchman, and for the first twelve years of their marriage the pair lived in Holland, where Betty worked as a nurse. One of her fondest memories of the country is ice skating. "I was perfectly all right," she laughs, "as long as my husband had a firm grip on me!"

What prompted this Harlequin author to start writing? It happened after she and Johannes left Holland for England; and Betty gives credit to a patron at a local library. "She complained that there weren't enough romantic novels to be found, and that clinched the matter for me."

With dozens of books behind her, Betty Neels has done much to correct that early complaint. "Mother's little hobby" has become "mother's profession," and thousands of devoted readers are grateful for that.

HARLEQUIN CLASSIC LIBRARY

Great old romance classics from our early publishing lists.

FREE BONUS BOOK

On the following page is a coupon with which you may order any or all of these titles. If you order all nine, you will receive a FREE book— *Doctor Bill*, a heartwarming classic romance by Lucy Agnes Hancock.

The thirteenth set of nine novels in the **HARLEQUIN CLASSIC LIBRARY**

Great old favorites...
Harlequin Classic Library
Complete and mail this coupon today!

FREE BONUS BOOK

Harlequin Reader Service

In U.S.A.
440 South Priest Drive
Tempe, AZ 85281

In Canada
649 Ontario Street
Stratford, Ontario N5A 6W2

Please send me the following novels from the Harlequin Classic Library. I am enclosing my check or money order for $1.50 for each novel ordered, plus 75¢ to cover postage and handling. If I order all nine titles at one time, I will receive a FREE book, *Doctor Bill,* by Lucy Agnes Hancock.

☐ 109   ☐ 112   ☐ 115
☐ 110   ☐ 113   ☐ 116
☐ 111   ☐ 114   ☐ 117

Number of novels checked @ $1.50 each =	$_____
N.Y. and Ariz. residents add appropriate sales tax	$_____
Postage and handling	$_____ .75
TOTAL	$_____

I enclose _____
(Please send check or money order. We cannot be responsible for cash sent through the mail.)
Prices subject to change without notice.

Name _____
(Please Print)

Address _____
(Apt. no.)

City _____

State/Prov. _____

Zip/Postal Code _____
Offer expires August 31, 1983   30556000000

ANTIGUA KISS
ANNE WEALE

The exciting new bestseller
by one of the world's top romance authors!

Christie's marriage to Caribbean playboy
Ash Lombard was to be for convenience only.
He promised never to touch her. That was fine
by Christie, a young widow whose unhappy first
marriage had destroyed the passionate side of
her nature—but it wasn't long before she
learned Ash had no intention of
keeping his word....

Available in January wherever paperback books are sold, **or** send your
name, address and zip or postal
code, along with a check or
money order for $3.70
(includes 75¢ for
postage and handling)
payable to Harlequin
Reader Service, to:

**Harlequin
Reader Service**

In the U.S.:
P.O. Box 22188
Tempe, AZ 85282

In Canada:
649 Ontario Street
Stratford, Ontario
N5A 6W2